A Transatlantic Tunnel, Hurrah!

A Transatlantic Tunnel, Hurrah!

by
HARRY HARRISON

Faber and Faber

London

First Published in Great Britain 1972 by
Faber and Faber Ltd
3 Queen Square, London WC1
Printed by Unwin Brothers Limited, Woking, Surrey
All rights reserved

ISBN 0 571 09996 3

All the characters and events portrayed in this story are fictitious. In this world. As for parallel worlds, we make no promises.

for
transatlantic
TOBY ROXBURGH
thespian, Savoyard, friend

Contents

BOOK THE THIRD
A STORM AT SEA

Book the First

The Link Between the Lands Begun

I. A HURRIED MESSAGE AND
A DANGEROUS MOMENT

Leaving Paddington Station, the *Flying Cornishman* seemed little different from any other train. Admittedly the appointments were cleaner and newer, and there was a certain opulence to the gold tassels that fringed the seat cushions in the first-class carriage, but these were just a matter of superficial decoration. The differences that made this train unique in England, which was the same as saying unique in the entire world, were not yet apparent as the great golden engine nosed its way over the maze of tracks and switches of the station yards, then out through the tunnels and cuttings. Here the roadbed was ordinary and used by all trains alike. Only when the hulking locomotive and its trailing cylinder of closely joined coaches had dived deep under the Thames and emerged in Surrey did the real difference show. For now even the roadbed became unusual, a single track of continuously welded rails on specially cushioned sleepers that was straighter and smoother than any track had ever been before, sparkling in deep cuttings that slashed a direct channel through the chalk of the downs, shooting arrow-straight across the streams on stumpy iron bridges, a no-nonsense rail line that changed direction only in the longest and shallowest of curves. The reason for this became quickly apparent as the acceleration of the train steadily increased until the nearby fields and trees flashed by, visible as just the most instantaneous of green blurs; only in the distance could details be picked out, but they too slipped backwards and vanished almost as soon as they had appeared.

Albert Drigg had the entire compartment to himself, and he was very glad of that. Although he knew that this train had made the return trip from Penzance every day for almost a

11

year now and had suffered no mishap, he was aware of this only in theory, so that now experiencing it in practice was a totally different matter. From London to Penzance was a total of 282 miles and that entire incredible distance would be covered in exactly two hours and five minutes—an average speed including stops of well in excess of 150 miles per hour. Was man meant to go that fast? Albert Drigg had a strong visceral sensation that he was not. Not even in this year of Our Lord 1973, modern and up to date though the empire was. Sitting so bolt upright in his black suit and black waistcoat that they showed no wrinkles, his stiff white collar shining, his gleaming leather portfolio on his knees, he generated no sign of his internal emotions. On the rack above, his tightly rolled umbrella and black bowler indicated he was a city man and men of the city of London are just not given to expressing their innermost feelings in public. Nevertheless he could not suppress a slight start when the compartment door whisked open on silent runners and a cheerful cockney voice addressed him.

"Tea, sir, tea?"

One hundred and fifty miles an hour—or more!—and the cup remained in place on the ledge beneath the window while the tea poured into it in a steady stream.

"That will be thrupence, sir."

Drigg took a sixpence from his pocket and passed it over to murmured thanks, then instantly regretted his largesse as the door closed again. He must be unnerved if he tipped in so magnanimous a manner, but he was solaced by the fact that he could put it on the expense account since he was traveling on company business. And the tea was good, freshly brewed and hot, and did very much to soothe his nerves. A whisky would do a lot more he realized, and he almost touched the electric button for the waiter when he remembered the Saloon Car, often seen in the pages of *The Tatler* and *Pall Mall Gazette*, but visited only by the very few. He finished the tea and rose, tucking the extra length of chain back into his sleeve. It bothered him that the portfolio was irremovably shackled to the cuff around his wrist and indicated that he was something less than a complete gentleman, but by careful maneuvering he could keep the chain from the public view. The Saloon Car, that was the very thing!

The carpeting in the corridor was a deep gold in color, making a subtle contrast with the ruddy, oiled gloss of the mahogany paneling. Drigg had to pass through another coach to reach the Saloon Car, but there was no need to struggle with recalcitrant doors as on an ordinary train, for as he approached, some ˜concealed device detected his proximity and the doors opened swiftly before him to the accompaniment of the hum of hidden electric motors. Naturally he did not look through the compartment windows he passed, but out of the corners of his eyes he had quick glimpses of finely dressed men and elegantly attired women, some children sitting sedately, reading—then a sudden loud barking that inadvertently drew his eye. Two country gentlemen sat with their feet up, emptying a bottle of port between them while a half dozen hounds of various breeds and sizes milled around and sought after their attention. And then Drigg was at the Saloon Car.

No automatic devices here but the best of personal services. A grand carved door with massive brass handles and a pillbox-capped boy, his double row of uniform buttons glinting and catching the eye, who saluted and tugged at the handles.

"Welcome, sir," he piped, "to the Grand Saloon Car of the London and Land's End Railway."

Now that he saw it in its full splendor Drigg realized that the newspaper photographs did not do the establishment justice. There was no feeling at all of being in a railway carriage, for the atmosphere was rather that of an exceedingly exclusive club. One side contained immense crystal windows, from floor to ceiling, framed by ruddy velvet curtains, while arrayed before them were the tables where the clientele could sit at their leisure and watch the rural countryside speeding by. The long bar was opposite, massed with ranked bottles that reflected in the fine cut-glass mirror behind it. There were windows to the right and left of the bar, delicately constructed stained-glass windows through which the sun poured to throw shifting colored patterns upon the carpet. No saints here, unless they be the saints of railroading, like Stephenson or Brunel, sturdy, far-seeing men with compasses and charts in hand. They were flanked by the engines of history with Captain Dick's Puffer and the tiny Rocket on the left, then progressing through history and time to the far right where the mighty atomic-powered Dreadnought appeared, the juggernaut of the rails that pulled this very train. Drigg sat near the window, his portfolio concealed beneath the table, and ordered his whisky, sipping at it slowly while he enjoyed the gay music-hall tune that a smiling musician was playing on the organ at the far end of the car.

This was indeed luxury, and he relished every moment of it, already seeing the dropping jaws and mute stares of respect when he told the lads about it back at The King's Head in Hampstead. Before he had as much as finished his first drink the train was easing to a stop in Salisbury, where he looked on approvingly as a policeman appeared to chase from the platform a goggling lot of boys in school jackets who stood peering into the car. His duty done, the officer raised his hand in salute to the occupants, then rolled majestically and flatfootedly on about his official affairs. Once more the *Flying Cornishman* hurled itself down the track, and with his second whisky Drigg ordered a plate of sandwiches, still eating them at the only other stop, in Exeter, while they were scarcely done before the train slowed for Penzance and he had to hurry back for his hat and umbrella.

The guards were lined up beside the locomotive when he passed, burly, no-nonsense-looking soldiers of the Argyll and Sutherland Highlanders, elegant in their dark kilts and white gaiters, impressive in the steadiness of their Lee-Enfield rifles with fixed bayonets. Behind them was the massive golden bulk of the Dreadnought, the most singular and by far the most powerful engine in the world. Despite the urgency of his mission Drigg slowed, as did all the other passengers, unable calmly to pass the gleaming length of her. Black driving wheels as tall as his head, drive rods thicker than his legs that emerged from swollen cylinders leaking white plumes of steam from their exhausts. She was a little travel-stained about her lower works, but all her outer skin shone with the seamless, imprisoned-sunlight glow of gold, fourteen-karat gold plating, a king's ransom on a machine this size. But it wasn't the gold the soldiers were here to guard, though that was almost reason enough, but the propulsive mechanism hidden within that smooth, unbroken, smokestackless shell. An atomic reactor, the government said, and little else, and kept its counsel. And guarded its engine. Any of the states of Germany would give a year's income for this secret while spies had already been captured who, it was rumored, were in the employ of the King of France. The soldiers sternly eyed the passersby, and Drigg hurried on.

The works offices were upstairs in the station building, and a lift carried him swiftly to the fourth floor. He was reaching for the door to the executive suite when it opened and a man emerged, a navvy from the look of him, for who else but a railway navvy would wear such knee-high hobnailed boots along with green corduroy trousers? His shirt was heavy canvas and over it he wore a grimy but still rainbow waistcoat, while around his pillarlike neck was wrapped an even gaudier handkerchief. He held the door but barred Drigg's way, looking at him closely with his pale-blue eyes which were startlingly clear in the tanned nutbrown of his face.

"You're Mr. Drigg, aren't you, sir?" he asked before the other could protest. "I've seen you here when they cut t'tape and at other official functions of t'line."

"If you please."

The thick-thewed arm still prevented his entrance, and there seemed little he could do to move it.

"You wouldn't know me, but I'm Fighting Jack, Captain Washington's head ganger, and if it's the captain you want t'see, he's not here."

"I do want to see him and it is a matter of some urgency."

"That'll be tonight then, after shift. Captain's up t'the face. No visitors. If you've messages in that bag, I'll bring 'em up for you."

"Impossible—I must deliver this in person." Drigg took a key from his waistcoat pocket and turned it in the lock of the portfolio, then reached inside. There was a single linen envelope there and he withdrew it just enough for the other to see the golden crest on the flap. Fighting Jack dropped his arm.

"The marquis?"

"None other." Drigg could not keep a certain smug satisfaction from his voice.

"Well, come along then. You'll have to wear overalls; it's mucky up t'face."

"The message must be delivered."

There was a work train waiting for the head ganger, a stubby electric engine drawing a single open car with boxes of supplies. It pulled out as soon as they were aboard, and they rode the footplate behind the engineer. The track passed the town, cut through the fields, then dived into a black tunnel where the only light was a weak glow from the illuminated dials so that Drigg had to clutch for support, fearful that he would be tossed out into the jolting darkness. Then they were in the sunshine again and slowing down as they moved toward a second tunnel mouth. It was far grander than the other with a facing of hewn granite blocks and marble pillars that supported a great lintel that had been done in the Doric style. This was deeply carved with the words that still brought a certain catch to Drigg's throat, even after all his years with the company.

TRANSATLANTIC TUNNEL they read.

Transatlantic tunnel—what an ambition! Less emotional men than he had been caught by the magic of those words, and even though there was scarcely more than a mile of tunnel behind this imposing façade, the thrill was still there. Imagination led one on, plunging into the earth, diving beneath the sea, rushing under those deep oceans of dark water for thousands of miles to emerge into the sunlight again in the New World.

Lights moved by, slower and slower, until the work train stopped before a concrete wall that sealed the tunnel like an immense plug.

"Last stop, follow me," Fighting Jack called out and swung down to the floor in a movement remarkably easy for a man his size. "Have you ever been down t'tunnel before?"

"Never." Drigg was ready enough to admit ignorance of this alien environment. Men moved about and called to one another with strange instructions; fallen metal clanged and echoed from the arched tunnel above them where unshielded lights hung to illuminate a Dante-ish scene of strange machines, tracks and cars, nameless equipment. "Never!"

"Nothing to worry you, Mr. Drigg, safe as houses if you do the right things at the right time. I been working on the railways and the tunnels all m'life, and outside of a few split ribs, cracked skull, a broken leg, and a scar or two, I'm fit as a fiddle. Now follow me."

Supposedly reassured by these dubious references, Drigg followed the ganger through a steel door set into the concrete bulkhead that was instantly and noisily slammed shut behind them. They were in a small room with benches down the middle and lockers on one wall. There was a sudden hissing and the distant hammering of pumps, and Drigg felt a strange pressure on his ears. His look of sudden dismay was noticed by Fighting Jack.

"Air, just compressed air, nothing more. And a miserable little twenty pounds it is, too, I can tell you, as one who has worked under sixty and more. You'll never notice it once you're inside. Here you go." He pulled a boiler suit from a locker and shook it out. "This is big enough to go over your clothes. I'll hold that wallet for you."

"It is not removable." Drigg shook out the length of chain for inspection.

"No key?"

"I do not possess it."

"Easily solved."

The ganger produced an immense clasp knife, with a swiftness and economy of motion that showed he had had sudden use for it before, and touched it so that a long gleaming blade shot out. He stepped forward and Drigg backed away.

"Now there, sir, did you think I was going to amputate? Just going to make a few sartorial alterations on this here garment."

A single slash opened the sleeve from wrist to armpit, and another twitch of the blade vented the garment's side. Then the knife folded and vanished into its usual resting place while Drigg drew on the mutilated apparel, the portfolio easily passing through the rent cloth. When Drigg had it on, Fighting Jack cut up another boiler suit—he had a cavalier

17

regard for company property apparently—and bound it around the cut sleeve to hold it shut. By the time this operation was completed the pumps had stopped and another door at the far end of the airlock room opened and the operator looked inside, touching his forehead when he saw Drigg's bowler.

A train of small hopper wagons was just emerging from a larger steel door in the bulkhead, and Fighting Jack pursed his lips to emit an ear-hurting whistle. The driver of the squat electric locomotive turned at the sound and cut his power.

"That's One-Eyed Conro," Fighting Jack confided to Drigg. "Terrible man in a dustup, thumbs ready all t'time. Trying to even the score, you see, for the one he had gouged out."

Conro glared out of his single reddened eye until they had climbed up beside him, then ground the train of wagons forward.

"And how's the face?" Fighting Jack asked.

"Sand." One-Eyed Conro spat a globe of tobacco juice into the darkness. "Still sand, wet sand. Loose at the top so Mr. Washington has dropped the pressure so she won't blow, so now there's plenty of water at the bottom and all the pumps is working."

" 'Tis the air pressure, you see," Fighting Jack explained to Drigg as though the messenger were interested, which he was not. "We're out under t'ocean here with ten, twenty fathoms of water over our heads and that water trying to push down through the sand and get t'us all the time, you see. So we raise the air pressure to keep it out. But seeing as how this tunnel is thirty feet high, there is a difference in the pressure from top to bottom and that's a problem. When we raise the pressure to keep things all nice at t'top, why then the water seeps in at t'bottom where the pressure is lower and we're like t'swim. But, mind you, if we was to raise the pressure so the water is kept out at t'bottom why then there is too much pressure at t'top and there is a possibility of blowing a hole right through to the ocean bottom and letting all the waters of the world down upon our heads. But don't you worry about it."

Drigg could do nothing else. He found that for some inexplicable reason his hands were shaking so that he had to grip the chain around his wrist tightly so it did not rattle. All too soon the train began to slow and the end of the tunnel appeared clearly ahead. A hulking metal shield that sealed off the workers from the virgin earth outside and enabled them to attack it through doorlike openings that pierced the steel. Drills were at work above, whining and grumbling, while mechanical shovels below dug at the displaced muck and loaded it into the waiting wagons. The scene appeared disorganized and frenzied, but even to Drigg's untutored eye it was quickly apparent that work was going forward in an orderly and efficient manner. Fighting Jack climbed down and Drigg followed him, over to the shield and up a flight of metal stairs to one of the openings.

"Stay here," the ganger ordered. "I'll bring him out."

Drigg had not the slightest desire to go a step farther and wondered at his loyalty to the company that had brought him this far. Close feet away from him was the bare face of the soil through which the tunnel was being driven.

Gray sand and hard clay. The shovels ripped into it and dropped it down to the waiting machines below. There was something sinister and frightening about the entire operation, and Drigg tore his gaze away to follow Fighting Jack who was talking to a tall man in khaki wearing high-laced engineer's boots. Only when he turned and Drigg saw that classical nose in profile did he recognize Captain Augustine Washington. He had seen him before only in the offices and at board meetings and had not associated that well-dressed gentleman with this burly engineer. But of course, no toppers here. . . .

It was something between a shout and a scream, and everyone looked in the same direction at the same instant. One of the navvies was pointing at the face of dark sand before him that was puckering *away* from the shield.

Blowout! someone shouted and Drigg had no idea what it meant except he knew something terrible was happening. The scene was rapid, confused, with men doing things and all the time the sand was moving away until suddenly a hole a good two feet wide appeared with a great sound like an immense whistle. A wind pulled at Drigg and his ears hurt, and to his horror he felt himself being drawn toward that gaping mouth. He clung to the metal in petrified terror as he watched strong

19

boards being lifted from the shield by that wind and being sucked forward, to splinter and break and vanish into oblivion.

A navvy stumbled forward, leaning back against the suction, holding a bale of straw up high in his strong arms. It was Fighting Jack, struggling against the thing that had suddenly appeared to destroy them all, and he raised the bale which was sucked from his grasp even as he lifted it. It hit the opening, was pressed flat, and hung there for an instant—then disappeared.

Fighting Jack was staggering, reaching for support to pull himself back to safety, his hand out to a steel bulkhead. His fingers were almost touching it, tantalizingly close, but he could not reach it. With a bellow, more of annoyance than fear, he rocked backwards, was lifted to his feet and dragged headfirst into the opening.

For one, long, terrifying moment he stuck there, like a cork in a bottle, just his kicking legs projecting into the tunnel.

Then he was gone and the air whistled and howled freely again.

II. A MOMENTOUS DECISION

All of the navvies, not to mention Albert Drigg, stood paralyzed by horror at the swiftness of the tragedy. Even these strong men, used as they were to a life of physical effort and hardship, accidents and sudden maiming, were appalled by the swiftness of the event. Only one man there had the presence of mind to move, to act, to break the spell that bound all of the others.

"To me," Captain Washington shouted, jumping to a bulwark of timbers that had been prepared for just this sort of emergency. Lengths of thick boards that were bolted to stout timbers to make a doorlike shield that stood as high as a man. It looked too heavy for one person to budge, yet Washington seized the edge and with a concerted contraction of all his muscles dragged it forward a good two feet.

His action jolted the others into motion, rallying to him to seize the construction and lift it and push it forward. The pressure of the air tore it from their hands and slammed it against the face of the cutting, covering the blowout opening at last. There was still the strong hiss of air pushing through the cracks in the boards, but the rushing torrent had now abated. Under Washington's instructions they hurried to contain and seal off the disaster. While above them, through the largest opening in the tunneling shield, a strange machine appeared, pushed forward by smoothly powerful hydraulic cylinders. It was not unlike a battleship gun turret, only in place of the cannon there were four long tubes that ended in cutting heads. These were placed against the sand above the blowout and instantly began revolving under the operator's control. Drilling swiftly, they sank into the soft sand until the turret itself was flush against the face of the cutting. As soon as this was done the drilling stopped and valves were opened—and an instant frosting of ice appeared upon the turret.

While this was happening, a brawny navvy with an ax had chopped a hole in the center of the wooden shield just over the opening of the blowout. The pressure was so strong that, when he holed through, the ax was torn from his hands and vanished. He stumbled back, laughing at the incident and holding up his hands so his butties could see the raw stripes on his palms where the handle of the ax had been drawn from his tight grip. No sooner had he stepped aside than the mouth of a thick hose was placed over this new opening, and a pump started to throb.

Within seconds the high-pitched whistle of the escaping air began to die away. Ice now coated the formerly wet sand through which the blowout had occurred, and a chilling wave of cold air passed over them all. When the rushing wind had vanished completely, Washington ordered the pumping stopped, and their ears sang in the sudden silence. The sound of a bell drew their attention as Captain Washington spun the handle on the field telephone.

"Put me through on the radio link to the boat at once."

They all listened with a fierce intentness as contact was established and Washington snapped the single word, "Report." He listened and nodded, then called out to his intent audience.

"He is safe. Alive and well."

They cheered and threw their caps into the air and only desisted when he raised his hands for silence.

"They saw the blowout on the surface, blowing muck and spray forty feet into the air when it first holed through. They went as close as they dared to the rising bubbles then and were right on the spot when Fighting Jack came by. Rose right up into the air, they said, and they had him almost as soon as he fell back. Unconscious and undamaged and when he came to he was cursing even before he opened his eyes. Now back to the job, men; we have twelve feet more to go today."

As soon as the rhythm of the work had resumed, Captain

Washington turned to Drigg and put out his hand in a firm and muscular handshake.

"It is Mr. Drigg, isn't it? The marquis' private secretary?"

"Yes, sir, and secretary of the board as well."

"You have caught us at a busy moment, Mr. Drigg, and I hope you were not alarmed. There are certain inherent difficulties in tunneling, but as you have seen, they are not insurmountable if the correct precautions are taken. There is a trough in the ocean bottom above us at this spot; I doubt if more than five feet of sand separate us from the water. A blowout is always a possibility. But prompt plugging and the use of the Gowan stabilizer quickly sealed the opening."

"I'm afraid it is all beyond me," said Drigg.

"Not at all. Simple mechanics." There was a glint of true enthusiasm in Captain Washington's eye as he explained. "Since the sand is watersoaked above us, the compressed air we use to hold back the weight of the water blew an opening right through to the sea bottom. The wooden barricade sealed the opening temporarily while the Gowan stabilizer could be brought up. Those drills are hollow, and as soon as they were driven home, liquid nitrogen was pumped through them. This fluid has a temperature of 345.5 degrees below zero, and it instantly freezes everything around it. The pipe you see there pumped in a slurry of mud and water which froze solid and plugged the opening. We shall keep it frozen while we tunnel past this dangerous area and seal it off with the cast-iron sections of tunnel wall. All's well that ends well—and so it has."

"It has indeed, and for your head ganger as well. How fortunate the boat was nearby."

Washington looked at the other keenly before answering. "Not chance at all, as I am sure you know. I do believe the last letter from the directors drawing my attention to the wasteful expense of maintaining the boat at this station was over your signature?"

"It was, sir, but it appeared there only as the drafter of the letter. I have no responsibility in these matters, being just the vehicle of the directors' wishes. But with your permission I shall give a complete report of what I have seen today and will stress how a man's life was saved because of your foresight."

"Just good engineering, Mr. Drigg."

"Foresight, sir, I insist. Where you put a man's life ahead of money. I shall say just that, and the matter will be laid to rest once and for all."

Washington seemed slightly embarrassed at the warmth in Drigg's voice, and he quickly sought to change the subject.

"I have kept you waiting too long. It must have been a matter of some importance that has brought you personally all this distance."

"A communication, if you please."

Drigg unlocked the portfolio and took out the single envelope it contained. Washington raised his eyebrows slightly at the sight of the golden crest, then swiftly broke the seal and read the letter.

"Are you aware of the contents of this letter?" said Washington, drawing the folded sheet of paper back and forth between his fingers.

"Only that the marquis wrote it himself and instructed me to facilitate in every way your return to London on a matter of some importance. We will be leaving at once."

"Must we? The first through connection on an up train is at nine, and it won't arrive until the small hours."

"On the contrary," Drigg said, smiling. "A special run of the *Flying Cornishman* has been arranged for your convenience and should be now waiting."

"It is that urgent then?"

"The utmost—His Lordship impressed that upon me most strongly."

"All right then, I will have to change. . . ."

"Permit me to interrupt. I believe instructions were also sent to the head porter of your hotel and a packed bag will be awaiting aboard the train."

Washington nodded acceptance; the decision had been made. He turned around and raised his voice over the growing din. "Bullhead. You will be head ganger here until Fighting Jack returns. Keep the work moving."

There was no more to be done. Washington led the way back through the shield to the electric locomotive which he commandeered for the return trip. They took it as far as the bulkhead and arrived just in time to meet Fighting Jack emerging from the airlock door.

"Damn me if I want to do that again," he bellowed, his clothes still dripping wet, bruises on his head and shoulders where he had been dragged through the ocean bottom. "Like a cork in a bung I was, stuck and thought it me last moments. Then up like a shot and everything getting black and the next I know I'm looking up t'sky and at the faces of some ugly sinners and wondering if I were t'heaven or the other place."

"You were born to be hanged," said Washington calmly. "Back to the face now and see they work the shift out without slackening."

"I'll do that and feed any man who shirks into a blowout and up the way I went."

He turned and stamped off while they entered the airlock and found seats.

"Should he be working . . . ?" Drigg ventured after long minutes of silence.

"He shouldn't—but I cannot stop him. These navvies have a way of life different from ours, and we must respect it. If he's hurt or has the bends, he would never admit it, and the only way to get him to hospital would be to bash him over the head, and he would never forgive me. I have seen these men, on a dare, jump over the open mouth of a ventiliation tunnel ten feet wide and a hundred feet deep. I have seen three men in a row fail and fall to their deaths and the fourth man, laughing, succeed. Then he and all the others there go out and drink beer until they can no longer walk in memory of their dead butties. And no one regretting or worrying about a thing. A hard and brutal life you might say, but by God it makes men."

As though ashamed of this emotional outburst, Washington kept his counsel for the rest of the trip out of the tunnel, until they reached the platform in Penzance. It was dark now with the last bars of red fading from the clouds in the west. Lights were winking on all over the expanse of tracks as the yardboys went about refilling the switch beacons with paraffin and lighting their wicks. The crowds were gone, the station silent, while the solitary form of the Dreadnought bulked even larger than life with its newly polished golden cladding catching and holding the red and green of the switch lights. There were only two carriages attached, the Saloon Car and Monarch of the Glens, the private coach used only by the marquis or other members of the board of directors. The porter for this car, an elderly white-haired man named Walker, formerly the butler of one of the board members, now retired to this sinecure in his advancing years, was waiting at the steps to the car.

"Your bath is drawn, sir, and your clothing laid out."

"Capital—but I must have a drink first. Join me if you will, Mr. Drigg; it has been a long and hot day with more than enough excitement for a month."

"A pleasure."

The gaudily uniformed boy was at the door to the Saloon Car, smiling as he drew it open for him. Washington stopped short when he saw him. "Should not this infant be in bed? Goodness knows we can open the door ourselves on this special trip."

The child's face fell and his lower lip showed a tendency to wobble before Drigg spoke. "They are volunteers all, Captain Washington, Billy here along with the rest. They want to go, you must understand that."

"Then go we shall." Washington laughed and entered the car. "Send a lemonade out to Billy, and we will all have that drink."

The organist looked over his shoulder, smiling out a fine display of gold teeth, and enthusiastically played "Pack Up Your Troubles" as soon as they entered. Washington sent him over a pint of beer, then raised his own and drained it in almost a single swallow. The train slipped forward so smoothly that they were scarcely aware that they were under way.

What with a few drinks and bathing and dressing, the trip was over almost before Washington knew it. The platform at Paddington Station was empty except for the shining eighteen-foot-long, six-doored, black form of a Rolls-Royce waiting for them. The footman held the door, and as soon as they were inside and he had joined the chauffeur they were in motion again. Around Hyde Park and up Constitution Hill past Buckingham Palace—windows all aglitter with a ball or some important function—and within short minutes they were pulling up in front of Transatlantic House, the company offices in Pall Mall. The front doors were held open, and not a word was spoken as Drigg led the way to the lift and up to the library. They stood there in the silence of morocco and dark wood until the porter had closed the outer door, and only then did Drigg touch a hidden catch on one of the shelves of books. An entire section of shelving opened like a door and he pointed through it.

"His Lordship is waiting in his private office. He thought to have a word with you alone before you go in to the board. If you will." Washington stepped forward while the secret doorway closed behind him and another door opened before.

The marquis was writing at his desk and did not at first look up. This was an elegant room, rich with silver and brass and heavy with ancestral portraits. Behind the marquis the curtains were open so the large bay window framed the view across St. James's Park with the tower of Big Ben visible beyond. As it solemnly struck the hour, the marquis laid down his pen and waved Washington to the nearby chair.

"It is a matter of some urgency," said he, "or I would not have rushed you away from your work in this cavalier manner."

"I realized that from the tone of your note. But you did not say what the matter was."

"We'll come to that in a moment. But I have asked you here, to see me alone, on what, for lack of a better term, might be called a personal matter."

His Lordship seemed ill at ease. He tented his fingers together before him, then dropped them flat, rubbed at the wide jaw so typical of his line, then turned around to look out the window, then swung around again.

"This is difficult to say, Captain Washington, and has to do with our respective families. We have ancestors, there might be ill-will, don't mean to infer, but you understand."

Washington did understand and felt some of the same embarrassment as the marquis. He had lived with this burden all his life so was better able to face it. Perhaps it would be best to have it out in the open than kept as a guilty secret.

"What is past is past," said he. "It is a matter of history and common knowledge that the first Marquis Cornwallis executed my ancestor George Washington as a traitor. I feel no shame at the fact, nor any personal animosity toward you or your family; you may take my word on that. The Battle of Lexington was fairly fought and fairly won and the Continental Army defeated. The first marquis was a soldier and could do no more than obey his orders, no matter how distasteful he found them personally. As you know, it was the king himself who ordered the execution. George Washington was a traitor—but only because he lost. If he had won, he would have been a patriot, and he deserved to win because his cause was a just one."

"I'm afraid I'm not so well read up on that period of history," Cornwallis said, looking down at his desk.

"You will excuse my outspokenness, Your Lordship, but this is something very close to me. Because of the revolt and the ill feelings that followed after it in the American colonies, we remain a colony to this day. While others, Canada and Australia, for example, have attained to full independent dominion status within the empire. You had better know that I am active in the independence movement and will do everything I can to hurry the day when Her Majesty will approve that status."

"I could not agree more warmly, sir! As you undoubtedly know, I am a man of firm Tory persuasion and strongly back my party's position that dominion status be granted in the manner you say."

He rose and pounded the desk soundly as he said this, then extended his hand to the other, a social grace he had chosen to ignore when Washington had entered, undoubtedly because of the delicate nature of their familial relationship. Washington could do no less, so he stood and shook the hand firmly. They stood that way for a long moment, then the marquis dropped his eyes and released Washington's hand, coughing into his fist to cover his embarrassment at this unexpected display of emotion. But it had cleared the air for what was to come.

"We are upon difficult times with the tunnel, Washington, difficult times," said Cornwallis, and his expression became as difficult as the times he alluded to, with his forehead furrowed as a ploughed field, the corners of his mouth drooping so far that his ample jowls fell an inch. "This immense project has worn two faces since the very beginning, and the private face is the one I allude to now. I am sure that you have some idea of the intricate financing of an enterprise this size, but I do not think you are aware of how political in nature the major considerations are. In simple—this is a government project, a sort of immense works program. You are shocked to hear this?"

"I must admit, sir, that I am, at the minimum, surprised."

"As well you might be. This country and its mighty empire are built upon the sound notion that strong men lead while others follow, weak men and inept corporations go to the wall, while the government and the crown keeps its nose out of private affairs. Which is all well and good when the economic weather is fair and the sun of the healthy pound beams down upon us all. But there are clouds across the face of that sun now, as I am sure you are well aware. While the frontiers were expanding, England grew fat with the wealth of the East India Company, the Hudson's Bay Company, the Inca-Andean Company, and all the others flowing our way. But I am afraid the last frontier has been pushed back to the final ocean and a certain placidity has settled upon the world and its economy. When businesses can no longer expand, they tend to contract and this industrial contractionism is rather self-perpetuating. Something had to be done to stop it. More men on the dole every day, workhouses full, charities stretched to the limit. Something, I say, had to be done. Something was done. Certain private businessmen, certain great corporations, met *in camera* and—with considerable reluctance I can assure you—decided that the overall solution of the problem was beyond them. Learned specialists in the field of economics were drawn into the discussions and at their insistence the still highly secret meetings were enlarged to include a committee from the Parliament. It was then that the tunnel project was first voiced, a project large enough to affect and stimulate the entire economy of both Britain and the American colonies. Yet its very size was its only draw-back; not enough private capital could be raised to finance it. It was then that the final, incredible step was taken. Crown financing would be needed." He lowered his voice unconsciously. "The queen was consulted."

This was a revelation of a staggering nature, a secret of state so well kept that Washington, privy as he was to the innermost operations of The Transatlantic Tunnel Company, had no slightest intimation of the truth until this moment. He was stunned at first, then narrowed his eyes in thought as he considered the ramifications. He was scarcely aware that the marquis rose and poured them each a sherry from the cut crystal decanter on the sideboard, though his fingers took it automatically and raised it to his lips.

He finally spoke. "Can you tell me what is the degree of involvement of the government?"

"In for a penny, in for a pound. Private investors have so far subscribed about twelve percent of the needed sum. Her Majesty's government has agreed to take eighty percent—but no more."

"Then we are eight percent short of our goal?"

"Precisely." The marquis paced the length of the room and back, his hands clasped behind him and kneading each other. "I've had my doubts from the beginning, God knows we have all had our doubts. But it was Lord Keynes who had his way, the queen's adviser, author of I don't know how many books on economics, ninety years if he is a day and still spry enough to take on all comers. He had us all convinced; it sounded so good when he told us how well it would work. Money in circulation, capital on the move, healthy profits for investors, businesses expanding to meet the needs for building the tunnel, employment all around, pay packets going out to the small merchants, a healthy economy."

"All of those things could be true."

"Damme, all those things *will* be true—if the whole thing doesn't go bust first. And it will go bust and things will be back to where they were if not worse unless we can come up with the missing eight percent. And, you will pardon my frankness, my boy, but it is your bloody fellow colonials who are tugging back on the reins. You can help us there, possibly only you can help us there. Without overexaggerating I can say the fate of the tunnel depends upon you."

30

"I will do whatever is needed, sir," Washington said quietly and simply. "You may count upon me."

"I knew I could or I would not have had you here. Forgive my bad manners, been a deucedly long day and more to come. We have an agreement with your colonial Congress and the governor general—yes, they were consulted, too; your economy shares the same debilitations as ours—to match equally all monies raised by private investors in the Americas. There has been but a trickle where we needed a flood. Radical changes are needed. You, of course, know Rockefeller, chairman of the American board, and Macintosh, Brassey-Brunel's agent in charge of the construction at the American end. Both have agreed, in the course of the greater good, that they will step down. The two positions will be combined into one, and you will be nominated tonight to fill it."

"Good God!" Washington gasped.

"May He approve and be on our side. Our first consideration was that the candidate be a good engineer, and you are that. We know you will do the work. The second is that you are a colonial, one of their own people, so the operation has a definite American ring to it. I realize that there are some among the Tories who hold your family name anathema—we must be frank—but I feel they are in a minority. Our hope is that this appointment and your efforts will spur the lagging sales of bonds that will permit the operation to continue. Will you do it?"

"I gave my word; I will not withdraw it now. But there will be difficulties."

"A single difficulty, and you can put the name to it."

"Sir Isambard. The design of the tunnel is all his, the very conception indeed. I am just an employee carrying out his orders as is his agent Macintosh, who is not even an engineer. If I am to assume this greater responsibility, I will be something close to his equal in all matters. He is not going to like it."

"The understatement of the century, my boy. He has been sounded out cautiously already with the predictable results." A light flashed on the desk and was accompanied by a soft beeping sound. "The board has returned after their dinners, and I must join them since no one is to know I have seen you. If you will be so kind as to wait in the library, you will be sent for. If matters go as we have planned, and they will since we have the votes, you will be sent a note outlining these proposals and then called before the board. There is no other way."

The door opened at a touch of a button on the desk, and Washington found himself back in the library.

There was a soft leather armchair there that he sank into gratefully and when, a few minutes later, Drigg came to inquire if he needed anything, he was deep in thought and roused up only long enough to shake his head in the negative. For this was without a doubt the pinnacle of his career—if only he could scale it. Yes, he could, he had no doubts about that, had been without doubts since he had left Mount Vernon for the last time, waving good-bye to his mother and sister at the gate of the simple cottage that was their ancestral home. A cottage that had been built in the shadow of the ivy-grown ruins of that greater house burned by the Tory mobs. He was already an engineer then, graduated first in his class from MIT despite the dishonor attached to his name—or perhaps because of it. Just as he had fought many a dark and silent battle with his fists behind the dorms, so had he fought that much harder contest in school to stay ahead, to be better, fighting with both his fists and his mind to restore honor to his family name. After graduation he had served his brief stint in the Territorial Engineers—without the ROTC grant he would never have finished college—and in doing so had enjoyed to its utmost his first taste of working in the field. There had been the usual troubles at the western frontier with the Spanish colonies so that the colonial authorities in New York had decided that a military railroad was needed there. For one glorious year he had surveyed rights of way through the impassable Rocky Mountains and labored in the tunnels that were being driven through the intractable rock. The experience had changed his life, and he had known just what he wanted from that time on. Along with the best minds from all the far-flung schools of the empire he had sat for the prestigious George Stephenson

32

scholarship at Edinburgh University and had triumphed. Acceptance had meant automatic entrance into the higher echelons of the great engineering firm of Brassey-Brunel, and this too had come to pass. Edinburgh had been wonderful, despite the slightly curled lips of his English classmates toward his colonial background, or perhaps because of this. For the first time in his life he was among people who attached no onus to his name; they could not be expected to remember the details of every petty battle fought at the fringes of their empire for the past four hundred years. Washington was just another colonial to be classified with Hindoos, Mohawks, Burmese, Aztecs, and others, and he reveled in this group anonymity.

His rise had been brief and quick, and now he was reaching the summit. Beware lest he fall when his reach exceeded his grasp. No! He knew that he could handle the engineering, drive the American end of the tunnel just as he was driving the British one. And though he was aware that he was no financier he also knew how to talk to the men with the money, to explain just what would be done with their funds and how well invested they would be. It would be Whig money he was after—though perhaps the Tories would permit greed to rise above intolerance and would climb on the bandwagon when they saw the others riding merrily away toward financial success.

Most important of all was the bearing this had upon a more important factor. Deep down he nursed the unspoken ambition to clear his family name. Unspoken since that day when he had blurted it out to his sister Martha and she had understood, when they had both been no more than children. Everything he accomplished, in some manner, reflected on that ambition, for what he accomplished in his own name was also done in the name of that noble man who had labored so hard for his country, who in return for his efforts was felled by a volley of English bullets.

"Captain Washington, Captain Washington, sir."

The voice penetrated the darkness of his thoughts, and as it did, he realized he had been hearing it for some time and not heeding. He started and took the envelope that Drigg held out to him, opened it and read it, then read it a second time more slowly. It was as Lord Cornwallis had said—the motion had been passed; he was being offered the post.

"If you will come with me, sir."

He rose and brushed the wrinkles from his waistcoat and buttoned his jacket. With the note still in his hand he followed the secretary to the boardroom to stand at the foot of the long dark table. The room was silent, all eyes upon him, as Cornwallis spoke from his place at the head of the table.

"You have read and understood our communication, Captain Washington?"

"I have, sir. It appears to be a request to fill, in a single capacity, the dual positions now occupied by Sir Winthrop and Mr. Macintosh. You indicate that these gentlemen approve of the change?"

"They do."

"Then I am most pleased to accept—with but one reservation before I do. I would like to know Sir Isambard's feelings on the change."

It was the waving of a red flag to a bull, the insulting of the queen to a loyal Englishman, the use of the word "frog" to a Frenchman. Sir Isambard Brassey-Brunel was on his feet in the instant, leaning both fists hard on the polished rosewood of the table, fire in his eye and white anger in the flare of his nostril. A small man before whom, in his anger, large men trembled, yet Washington was not trembling because perhaps he was not the trembling type. A study in opposites they were, one tall, one slight, one middle-aged and smooth of skin whose great breadth of forehead grew greater with the passing days, the other with a forehead of equal magnitude but with a face browned and lined by sun and wind. A neatly turned-out English gentleman from the tips of his polished, handcrafted boots to the top of his tonsured head—with a hundred guineas of impeccable Savile Row tailoring in between. A well-dressed colonial whose clothes were first class yet definitely provincial, like the serviceable and rugged boots intended more for wear than show.

"You wish to know my feelings," Sir Isambard said, "you wish to know my feelings." The words were spoken softly yet could be heard throughout all of that great room and perhaps because of this gentleness of tone were all the more ominous. "I will tell you my feelings, sir, strong feelings that they are, sir. I am against this appointment, completely against it and oppose it, and that is the whole of it."

"Well then," Washington said, seating himself in the chair placed there for his convenience. "That is all there is to it. I cannot accept the appointment."

Now the silence was absolute, and if a silence could be said to be stunned, this one certainly was. Sir Isambard was deflated by the answer, his anger stripped from him, and as anger, like air from a balloon, leaked from him he also sank slowly back into his seat.

"But you have accepted," Cornwallis said, baffled, speaking for all of them.

"I accepted because I assumed the board was unanimous in its decision. What is proposed is a major change. I cannot consider it if the man by whom I am employed, the master architect of this construction, the leading engineer and contractor in the world, is against it. I cannot, in all truth, fly in the face of a decision like that."

All eyes were now upon Sir Isambard whose face was certainly a study worth recording in its rapid changes of expression that reflected the calculations of the mighty brain behind it. First anger, giving way to surprise, followed by the crinkling forehead of cogitation and then the blankness of conclusion ending with a ghost of a smile that came and went as swiftly as a passing shadow.

"Well said, young Washington; how does it go? You shall not speak ill of me—I am your friend, faithful and just upon you. I detect the quality of your classical education. The burden of decision now rests upon my shoulders alone and I shall not shirk it. I have the feeling that you know more of these matters than you intimate; you have been spoken to or you would not be so bold. But so be it. The tunnel must go through and to have a tunnel we apparently have to have you. I withdraw my objections. You are a good enough engineer I must admit, and if you follow orders and build the tunnel to my design, we will build well." He reached out his small, strong hand to take up a glass of water, the strongest spirit he ever allowed himself, while something like a cheer echoed from all sides. The chairman's gavel banged through the uproar, the meeting was concluded, the decision made, the work would go on. Sir Isambard waited stolidly to one side while the members of the board congratulated Washington and one another, and only when the engineer was free did he step to his side.

"You will share a cab with me." It was something between a request and a command.

"My pleasure."

They went down in the lift together in silence and the porter opened the door for them and whistled for a cab. It was a hansom cab, two-wheeled, high, black, and sleek, the driver perched above with the reins through his fingers, these same reins leading down to one of the new-fangled conversions that were slowly removing the presence of the horse from central London. Here there was no proud, high-stepping equine frame between the shafts, but instead a squat engine of some sort whose black, metal, bricklike form rested upon three wheels. The single front wheel swiveled at a tug upon the reins bringing the hansom up smartly to the curb, while a tug on another rein stopped the power so it glided to a halt.

"An improvement," Sir Isambard said as they climbed in. "The horse has been the bane of this city—droppings, flies, disease, but no more. His replacement is quiet and smoothly electric powered with no noise or noxious exhaust like the first steam models, batteries in the boot—you will have noticed the wires on the shafts. Now close that trap because it is privacy not eavesdropping we want."

This last was addressed to the round and gloomy face of the cabby who peered down through the opening from above like a misplaced ruddy moon.

"Begging your pardon, your honor, but I've not heard the destination."

"One hundred and eight Maida Vale." The slam of the hatch added punctuation to his words, and he turned to Washington. "If you had supposed you were returning with me to my home, dispel yourself of the idea at once."

"I had thought. . . ."

"You thought wrong. I wished only to talk with you in

private. In any case, Iris is at some sort of theological tomfoolery at Albert Hall this evening, so we can be spared any scenes. She is my only daughter and she obeys me when she must, but she also shares my views of the world. When I explain to her that you have joined with my antagonists on the board to deprive me of my full responsibilities, that you now may wish to obtain my position for yourself—"

"Sir!"

"Be quiet. This is a lecture, not a discussion. That you have taken the position occupied by one of my agents and have completely turned against me. When I tell her those things, she will understand at once why I will bar my house from you in the future and she will return your ring to your club by messenger in the morning. We will continue our business relationship because there is no other way. But your engagement to my daughter is broken, you are no longer welcome in my home, and you will make no attempts, now or in the future, to contact Iris." He knocked loudly on the hatch with the head of his cane. "Stop the cab. Good-bye."

III. THE ROYAL ALBERT HALL

A fine rain was falling, darkening even more the black pavement of Kensington Gore so that each yellow gaslight above had its mirror-imaged fellow beaming back at it from the street below. The doors to the hall were closed, the street empty save for a single figure that appeared suddenly around the corner, a gentleman in a hurry and heedless of the inclemencies of the weather, his hat and clothes bedewed with raindrops. Taking the steps two at a time, he threw open one of the outer doors of the hall and came face to face with the ample, uniformed figure of the commissionaire who prevented any further forward motion by the sheer bulk of his presence.

"Performance begun, sir. Everyone seated."

"I wish to talk to someone in the audience," said Washington while at the same time forcing himself into some form of composure, realizing that his sudden appearance out of the night might be misinterpreted. "It is a matter of some urgency—I'll purchase a ticket if necessary."

"Dreadfully sorry, sir. Ticket window closed."

Washington already had his purse in his hand as these words were spoken which led naturally to a further and hopefully more successful attempt at entry. He slipped two half crowns into his hand.

"Are you sure there is no way? Perhaps I could just step inside and look around for my party?" There was a glint of silver that although instantly vanished still seemed to work a miraculous change on the doorkeeper's manner, for he stepped back and waved entrance with his hand.

"Perfectly understandable, sir. Walk this way."

The door closed silently behind his back, and Washington

looked around the partially filled hall. In the darkness he could make out only the fact that the audience seemed to be almost completely female, and he wondered how he could possibly single out one singular and important female from all the others. They were listening in rapt silence to a small man with a gray beard and black skullcap who stood at the lectern on the platform. Behind him, incongruously enough, there was a red plush divan upon which lay a rather fat and ordinary-looking woman who was either unconscious or sleeping. The juxtaposition of this strangely matched pair was so arresting that, with no opportunity at the moment for seeking out Iris from the audience, despite himself, Washington found himself listening to the speaker.

". . . have heard what Madame Clotilda has said, spoken the name Martin Alhaja Gontran, almost, in the fulsomeness of her experience, shouted this name signifying the importance of said name. This relates to what I have spoken of earlier in the outlining of my theory of the multiserial nature of time. There are these points in time which I have named alphanodes, and it is upon the existence of these alpha-nodes that my theory depends. If they exist, my theory has some validity and may be explored; if they do not exist, then time flows on like a river, a single mighty stream, instead of the multibranching, parallel rivulets that I postulate. If the alpha-nodes are not there, then I am wrong."

"Hear, hear," Washington said under his breath, searching for a singular dark and lovely head among all the rows of possibly dark and lovely heads before him.

"The search for a major alpha-node has taken years, and Madame Clotilda is the first clairvoyant to have made contact, so difficult is the task. At first, with the greatest difficulty, she spoke the single word *Gontran*, and I searched long and deep for the meaning. I thought I had found the correct reference, and tonight before you it has been revealed that I was correct, for when I said *Martin* she supplied the missing third part. Alhaja! The name, the all-important complete name that pinpoints with exactitude our alpha-node. Martin Alhaja Gontran. Let me tell you who he was, this unimportant little man, this illiterate shepherd who held the creation of an entire world in the palm of his cracked and calloused hand. I ask you to consider the date, the sixteenth of July in the year 1212. The scene is the Iberian peninsula, and a mighty battle is in preparation between the Christian and the Moslem forces. They lie under arms in their separate camps, the watchfires burn low; they gather their strength for the battle of the morrow. But all are not asleep. This shepherd, this Martin Alhaja Gontran, has spoken to a friend about what he has planned to do, and the friend has spoken to certain others and Gontran is apprehended by the Moors. These were uncivilized times and men did wreak pain and suffering upon their fellowmen of a sort that I will not speak for the gentle ears of the members of the fairer inclination among my audience. Suffice to say, Gontran spoke before he died, and revealed the fact that he had planned to lead Christian troops that night by secret and unguarded paths that he knew of, being a shepherd, that would bring them behind the Muslim lines. He died and this was not done. Now I ask you consider what *might* have happened if he had succeeded in his plan. It is very possible that the Christians instead of the Muslims might have won the battle of Navas de Tolosa the following day, possibly the most decisive battle of the period. I ask you to speculate further. If they had won, they might have gone on to further victories, and the Iberian Peninsula might be another Christian country like France or Prussia, instead of being Muslim and part of the Greater Caliphate. Of what importance to us is this distant part of the continent you may ask, and I answer of the utmost because cause is linked invariably to event. Cause and event. With Christian rulers in Iberia. . . ."

Behind him on the platform the sturdy form of Madame Clotilda began to stir and move while from her throat there came a sound somewhere between a sigh and a muffled gasp. The greater part of the audience gasped in echo and stirred as well so that Dr. Mendoza had to raise his hands for silence.

"It is fine, it is normal, do not disturb yourselves I beg of you. See, the physician is here now, waiting ready in the wings in case of need. The strain upon the system is great for a clairvoyant, and sometimes, ha-ha, there is a little reaction which is quickly taken care of. See, the curtains close, the doctor is at her side, all will be well. I ask the houselights to be raised; I will return in a moment after a small intermission during which you will hear a recording of an Eskimo ritual chant I myself recorded in a winter camp of these hardy indigenes north of the Arctic Circle while determining the basic relationship of diurnal time to Circadian rhythms so important to the foundations of the alpha-node theory. I thank you."

With these words the lights came on, and the little doctor, after a brief struggle to find the opening in the curtain, vanished from sight while their ears were assaulted by an inhuman and high-pitched wailing mixed with a dull thudding. Washington seized the unexpected opportunity and hurried down the aisle, searching the audience for that certain face.

And there she was, in the second row, just in from the aisle, dark hair drawn back and held sweetly by a golden clasp, features perfect, for she was indeed a startling beauty whom the newspaper photographers loved to find at balls. Her lips were as full and red without the touch of artifice as any other girl's after labor at the paintpot. As always he was without words when he first looked at her, filled with happiness to be in her presence. But she must have felt his eyes upon her, for she glanced up, and her startled expression broke into a smile of such warmth that, if possible, his powers of speech were removed even further from accessibility.

"Why Gus, here! What a pleasant surprise." He smiled in response, capable of nothing more coherent. "Have you met Joyce Boardman? I don't think you have; she's just home from the Far East. Joyce, my fiancé, Captain Augustine Washington."

He took the offered hand, bowing slightly, vaguely aware of an attractive female presence, nothing more. "A pleasure. Iris, I hate to break in like this, but I've just come up from Cornwall and I'll be going back in the morning. Would it be possible to see you now, to talk to you?"

Other words were on her lips, but she must have detected something unusual in his manner or his voice, for she changed them before she spoke, and when she did so, it was with a firm decisiveness unusual in a girl just past twenty.

"Of course. Madame Clotilda's fainting spell seems to have

interrupted matters, and if the doctor does speak again, Joyce can tell me all about it tomorrow. That will be all right with you, won't it, Joyce dear?" Joyce dear had little chance to answer or protest because Iris went on in a rush of words perhaps to forestall any utterance of this type. "That's so kind of you. When the car comes, tell them I've already gone home by cab."

Then she was on his arm, and they were going up the aisle. While the commissionaire was calling a cab, Washington realized that the issue had to be faced at once.

"Before the cab comes, I must tell you—your father and I have had a difference of opinion."

"The easiest thing in the world to do. I am at it all the time. Poor daddy is certainly the firmest-minded man in the world."

"I'm afraid this is more serious. He has forbidden me the house and—this is even harder to say—does not want us to see each other ever again."

She was silent in thought for a long moment, and the happy smile slowly vanished from her face. But she held his arm no less tightly, for which he loved her, if it were possible, ever much the more.

"Then we shall talk about it, and you must tell me everything that has happened. We'll go—let me see—to the lounge in the Great Western Hotel at Paddington. It's on the way home, and I remember you liked the tea and cakes there."

In the privacy of the cab, while they crossed the rain-filled darkness of Hyde Park, he told her what had happened. Told her everything except the irrelevant details of his confidential talk with Cornwallis, explained why the appointment was being made and how important it was both to the company and to him, then closed by repeating almost word for word the final and decisive conversation with her father. When he had finished, they were already at the hotel and there was nothing more that could be said until they had climbed the grand staircase and been seated, ordered the tea and cakes, and it must be admitted a double brandy for him since he felt greatly in need of one, and the silence lasted until the tea had been poured.

"This is a terrible thing to have happen, Gus, a terrible thing."

"You don't think your father is right, do you?"

"I don't have to think whether he is right or not, I only have to remember that he is my father."

"Iris, darling, you can't mean that! You're a girl of the twentieth century, not a Victorian shadow of a woman. You have the vote now, or at least you will next year when you are of age; women have a freedom under Elizabeth they never knew before."

"We do, and I know it, and I do love you, dear Gus. But this cannot do away with my family ties. And you said it yourself, I have not attained my majority nor will I for six months and I still remain in my father's house."

"You can't mean—"

"But I do, and it hurts me to have to say it. Until you and daddy resolve this terrible thing that has come between you, I have only one thing I must do. Gus, darling Gus, I really have no choice."

There was a gasp and a welter of emotion in the last words she spoke, while a tear brimmed from the corner of each eye as she took the ring from the finger of her left hand and put it into his palm.

IV. ABOARD THE AIRSHIP

What a glorious June day it was. Excitement filled the streets of Southampton and washed like breaking waves along her docks. The weather smiled as did the people, calling out to one another, drifting by twos and threes down toward the waterfront and the rapidly approaching hour of noon. Gay bunting and bright flags snapped in the offshore breeze while small boats scudded over the placid surface of the harbor like water bugs. A sudden sense of urgency came unto the strollers and they moved slightly faster when the distant wail of a train's whistle sounded from the hills. The boat train from London; the passengers were here!

The echo of the whistle drew Gus Washington from the well of his work, away from the blueprints, charts, diagrams, figures, plans, devices, pounds, dollars, and worries that snapped up at him out of the welter of papers he had spread around the train compartment. He pinched at the bridge of his nose where a persistent pain of fatigue nibbled him, then rubbed his sore eyes. He had been doing a good deal, some would say too much, but it was just a great amount of work that could not be avoided. Well enough for the moment. The tracks curved down toward the docks and he folded the scattered papers and documents and put them back into his bulging case, a sturdy, no-nonsense, heavy-strapped and brass-buckled case of horsehide, pinto pony hide, to be exact, with the gay white and brown pattern of the hair still there, a pony he had once ridden and ridden well to a good cause in the Far West, but that is another story altogether. Now as he filled the case and sealed it the train rattled across the points and out along the quay and he had his first sight of the *Queen Elizabeth* tied up at her berth ahead.

This was a sight for sore eyes that rendered them pain-free upon the instant. This was a marvel of engineering, of technical skill and daring the like of which the world had never seen before. So white she glistened in the sun, her bow pressed against the wharf and her distant stern far out in the stream. The gangplank reached up to the foredeck where a Union Jack flew proudly from a flagstaff. Out, far out, to both sides stretched the immense wings, white and wide, with the impressive bulk of the engines slung beneath them. Four to each side, eight in all, each with a four-bladed propeller, each blade of which was taller than a man. The *Queen Elizabeth,* pride of the Cunard Line, the grandest and most glorious flying ship in existence. For six months she had been flying with her select crew, around the world, showing the flag in every ocean and on the shores of almost every land. If there had been any difficulties at all during this trial period, the company had kept them a close secret. Now her extended proving flight was over, and she would begin the run for which she had been designed, the prestigious North Atlantic route of the Queens, Southampton to New York nonstop, 3,000 miles or more. Nor was it any accident that Gus Washington was on this flight, a simple engineer who ranked almost at the foot of the passenger list, overshadowed by the dukes and lords, the moguls of industry, the handful of European nobility and the great, titled actor. One hundred passengers only and at least ten or a hundred applicants for every berth. There had been pressure in high places, quiet chats over port at certain clubs, discreet telephone calls. The affairs of the tunnel affected both high finance and the court, and both were in agreement that everything must be done to encourage the American financial cooperation in the venture. Washington must go to the colonies, so let him go in the most fitting manner, a style that guaranteed the maximum publicity for the trip.

The maiden voyage of the flying ship was opportunity knocking. Opportunity that was admitted even before she rapped, although it meant that Gus had to pack a fortnight's work into five days. It was done, he was ready, the voyage was at hand. He sealed his case and opened the compartment door and joined the other passengers on the platform. There were not many, and he held back so they could go ahead to the pop of flashbulbs and the click of the press cameras. Not all had come by train; the barrier that held back the swelling crowd was opened to admit two automobiles, high, black, ponderous Rolls-Royces. As it began to close behind them, there was an imperious blast of a steam whistle from the street beyond, and it hurriedly opened again to admit the extended form of a Skoda Steamer, a vehicle much favored by European royalty. It had six wheels, the rear driving pair almost twice the size of the two others, as well as a cabin to the rear that housed the engine and the stoker. It emitted a plume of steam again as its whistle sounded and it eased silently by, trailing a faint cloud of smoke, the stately figures inside framed by the silver-mounted windowframes looking neither to right nor left. This was indeed a day to be remembered.

Farther along the platform the station café was open, frequented apparently only by the press since the passengers appeared to be going directly aboard. Gus had a wonderfully cooling pint of bitter before he was recognized and collared by the gentlemen of the fourth estate. He talked with them easily and answered their questions about the tunnel frankly. Everything was fine, just fine, on schedule and forging ahead. The tunnel would be built, have no fear. They honored his request not to be photographed with the glass in his hand, since teetotal money was among the funds subscribed for the tunnel, and they accepted with thanks his offer of a round for all of them. The voyage was having an auspicious start.

When he emerged into the sunlight again, the gangplank was clear and the passengers all boarded. Gus in turn climbed to the foredeck and accepted the salute of the ship's officer waiting there, a salute that hesitated and stopped halfway up from the sharply creased uniform leg to the shining billed cap and turned suddenly into an outstretched hand ready to clasp his.

"Hawkeye Washington—that is you!"

The clock of time rolled back in that instant, and Gus was once more in digs at Edinburgh, in class, facing the driving rain while walking up Prince's Street. Hawkeye—legendary hero of a popular novel whose name was hung on most students from the American colonies. He smiled broadly and took the proffered hand and pressed it strongly.

"Alec, and that is you, isn't it, hiding behind all that RAF mustache? Alec Durell."

"None other, Hawkeye, none other. And it was earned the hard way, I must say," he said, touching the great sweep of the thing with his knuckle as he spoke of it. "Donkey's years in the RAF, then Fleet Air Arm, finally to Cunard when they swept the services for our best flying people."

"Still shy I see?"

"As ever. Lovely to have you aboard. Look, come on to the bridge and meet the boys. I'm first engineer. They're a good lot. All ex-services, only place the company could find the flyers to handle an ark like this. Not a real company man in the pack if you don't count the purser and he isn't allowed on the bridge."

They went aft but bypassed the passenger entrance just below the high windows of the bridge and entered through a small doorway in the hull marked CREW ONLY. This led to an ample chamber, windowed to the sides and front and filled with instruments and controls. The helmsman was seated the farthest forward, with the captain and the first officer to his right and left. To the rear were the open doors of the small cubicles of the radio operator and the navigator. The walls were teak paneled, the fascia for the instruments of walnut and chrome, while the floor was covered wall to wall with a fine Wilton carpet. All of the positions were vacant at the moment other than that of the helmsman on duty who sat, staring dutifully ahead, with his fingers resting lightly on the spokes of his steering wheel.

"Officers all below," said Alec. "Chatting up the first-class passengers as always. Praise be, I have my engines to look after, so I don't have to join them. I say, let me show you around the engine room; I think you'll enjoy that. Just bung your case into nav's cubby, all the room in the world in there."

The navigator might not think so; the room was scarcely larger than a phone box, and Gus had trouble finding a free corner for his case. Then Alec opened a hatch and led him down a spiral staircase to the forehold where longshoremen were putting aboard the last of the luggage, suitcases and great steamer trunks, lashing them into place with netting. A narrow walkway was left that they followed down the length of the vessel toward the stern.

"Passenger deck is one deck up, but we can avoid them by going this way." Voices could be heard dimly above them accompanied by the lively strains of a merrily playing band.

"It sounds like a ten-piece brass band up there—don't tell me you ship all of them along, too?"

"Only in the ethereal sense, tape recordings you know. Have to watch the gross weight; the ruddy thing runs over one hundred tons before she gets airborne."

"I seem to have noticed little concern for weight up until now."

"You can say that again—or tell it to the board of governors, if you will. In the Cunard tradition, they insist. If we stripped off all the chrome and brass and teak, we could get another hundred passengers aboard."

"Though not in the same comfort. Perhaps they want quality not quantity?"

"There is that. Not my worry. Here we go, into this lift, a tight fit for two, so try to think small." It operated automatically; the door closed and they rose smoothly at the touch of the button. "Wing is right on top of the body and this saves a climb."

They emerged inside a low-ceilinged passage that ran transverse to the length of the ship, with heavy doors sealing each end, knobs and indicator lights set into their frames. The engineer turned right and actuated the controls so the door there swung open to disclose a small room, little bigger than the lift they had just quitted.

"Airlock," he said as the door behind them closed and another before them opened. "No point in pressurizing the engine rooms so we do this instead. Welcome to the portside engine room of the *Queen Elizabeth,* where I rule supreme."

This rule was instantly challenged by a rating in a soiled white boilersuit who saluted indifferently then shook his thumb gloomily over his shoulder.

"Still at it, sir, fueling, topping up the bunkers they say."

"My orders were to have it done by ten."

"And that I've told them, sir," spoken with such an air of infinite sadness, as though all the woes of the ages rode the man's thin shoulders.

"Well, they'll hear them again," said the engineer and added a score of colorful oaths that indicated both his military as well as his nautical background. He stamped over to a large hinged plate in the floor, unlocked the handles that secured it, and threw it open. The water was a good twenty feet below as he seized the edge of the opening and popped his head and half of his upper body down through it so he hung upside-down. "Ahoy the barge," he bellowed.

Gus knelt at the opposite side where he had a perfect view of the proceedings. A hulking barge with a pumping station at one end was tied up against the hull of the *Queen Elizabeth*. Great pipes snaked up from it to valves inset in the ship's side, the last of which was even then being disconnected. As it came away, a great burst of black coal dust sullied the side of the leviathan of the air and the first engineer's comments entertained an even more colorful content. But as soon as all the pipes were away and the valves sealed, hoses were brought into play and within moments the hull was pristine again. Alec pulled himself back inside with a victorious gleam in his eye—then sprang forward to the engine room telegraph as its bell rang twice and the brass indicator arm moved all around the face then returned to *warm engines.*

"Port, one," Alec called out. "Butane inlet valves."

"Aye, aye," the rating answered, and the two men were instantly involved in the complex task.

Gus knew the theory, of course, but he had never seen one of these giant engines in operation before. He was aware that each of the hulking turboprop engines, only a fraction of which protruded up through the bottom of the wing that was the floor here, produced 5,700 horsepower. First butane was admitted as an electric motor started the great shaft spinning with a muffled roar. Now the burning gas spun the turbine blades, faster and faster, until the desired temperature and pressures had been reached. Alec tapped a dial and seemed satisfied, so he cut off the butane flow while at the same instant turning on the pump that blew the tiny particles of pulverized coal into the engine, where it burned instantly and hotly. The great machine trembled and rumbled with restrained power as he adjusted the controls so it idled smoothly.

"I'll be down here until well after we're airborne, still have to fire up the starboard lot. Why don't you go back to the bridge; I'll phone through and tell them you are on the way up."

"Surely that would be an interference?"

"Not a bit of it. For every question you ask about this airborne Moby Dick they'll have a dozen about your transatlantic pipe. Get along now."

The engineer was not far wrong, for the captain himself, Wing Commander Mason, met Gus and insisted he remain. The bridge was quiet, commands were issued in a restrained manner and obeyed with alacrity, so it appeared that all the excitement was outside. The dockside crowd was waving and cheering, boat whistles blowing, until just on the stroke of midday the lines were cast off and the tugs nosed the ponderous airship away from the shore and out into the channel. Mason, who was young for a Cunard captain but who had grown a full beard to fit the accepted image, was proud of his charge.

"Waterline weight one hundred and ninety-eight thousand pounds, Mr. Washington, two hundred and forty feet from stem to stern, seventy-two feet from the bottom of the step to the lookout's position top of the central tailfin. An exercise in superlatives, and all of them truthful, I must admit. We have a two thousand horsepower turbine in the tail that does nothing more than pump air for the boundary layer control and deflected slipstream, increases our lift to triple that of an ordinary wing. Why, we'll be airborne at fifty miles an hour and inside four hundred feet. Spray-suppressor grooves on both sides of the hull keep down the flying scud and smooth the sea for us. Now, if you will excuse me."

The tugs cast off, the helmsman spun the wheel to line the ship up for the takeoff, then disengaged his controls so the captain had command. Hooting police boats had cleared the harbor of small craft. Steadying the airborne tiller with his left hand the captain rang for *full ahead* with his right. A faint vibration in the deck could be felt as the turbines howled up to top speed and the *Queen Elizabeth* slipped forward over the water, faster and faster. The transition was so smooth that there was no distinction between being waterborne and airborne. In fact the very presence of this juggernaut of the airways was so solid and reassuring that it appeared as though instead of the ship rising, the city outside had dropped away from them, shrinking at the same time to the size of a model, then tipping on its side as the ship began a slow turn to the west. Below them now the Isle of Wight slipped by, an unimportant green scrap of flotsam in the sparkling ocean, then they were out over the channel with England contracting and vanishing under their starboard wing. Gus picked up his case and slipped below, happy to have shared this moment of triumph with these furrowers of a new and dimensionless sea.

A short corridor led aft to the Grand Saloon where the passengers were seeing and being seen. They sat at the tables, admired the view from the great circular ports, and gave the bar a brisk business. The room was not as spacious as its title indicated, but the dark, curved ceiling gave an illusion of size with its twinkling stars and drifting clouds projected there by some hidden device. Gus worked his way through the crowd until he caught the eye of a porter who led him to his cabin. It was tiny but complete, and he dropped into the armchair with relief and rested, looking out of the porthole for a while. His bags that were labeled "cabin" were there, and he knew that there were other papers in them that he should attend to. But for the moment he sat quietly, admiring the simplicity and beauty of the cabin's construction—it *was* an original Picasso lithograph on the wall—and the way the chair and desk would fold and vanish at night so the bunk could be opened. Eventually he yawned, stretched, opened his collar, opened his case, and set to work. When the gong sounded for luncheon, he ignored it but sent instead for a pint of draught Guinness and a plowman's lunch of bread, cheese, and pickles. On this simple fare he labored well, and by the time the gong sounded again, this time for dinner, he was more than willing to put his work away and join his fellowman. Even though it was a fellow woman who shared his table at the first seating, a lady of advanced years, very rich though of lowly antecedents. Both of these could be read easily into her jewelry and her vowels so that, eating swiftly, Gus returned to his cabin.

During his absence his bed had been opened and turned back, an electric hotwater bottle slipped between the sheets since the cabins were cooled to a refreshing sleeping temperature, and his pajamas laid across the pillow. Ten o'clock by his watch but—he spun it ahead five hours to New York time—they would be roused deucedly early. Three hundred miles an hour, a fifteen-hour flight. It might be a ten A.M. arrival local time, but it would be five A.M. to his metabolism, so he determined to get as much rest as possible. It was going to be a hectic day, week, month, year—hectic forever. Not that he minded. The tunnel was worth it, worth anything. He yawned, slipped between the covers, and turned off the light. He left the porthole curtains open so he could watch the stars moving by in stately splendor before he went to sleep.

The next sensation was one of struggling, drowning, not being able to breathe, dying, pinned down. He thrashed wildly, fighting against the unbreakable bands that bound him, trying to call out but finding his nose and mouth were covered.

It was not a dream. He had never smelled anything in a dream before, never had his nose assaulted in this manner; never had it been clogged with the cloying sweetness of ether.

In that instant he was wide awake, completely awake, and catching his breath, holding it, not breathing. In the Far West he had helped the surgeon many times, poured the ether into the cone on a wounded man's face, and had learned to hold his breath against the escaping, dizzying fumes. He did that now, not knowing what was happening but knowing that if he breathed in as much as one breath more he would lose consciousness.

There was no light, but as he struggled he became aware that at least two men were leaning their full weight on him, holding him down. Something cold was being fastened on his wrists while something else prisoned his ankles at the same time. Now the heavy figures simply held him while he writhed, keeping the ether rag to his face, waiting for him to subside.

It was torture. He fought on as long as he could before letting his struggles cease, went past the time where he wanted to breathe to the point where he needed to breathe to the excruciating, horrifying moment where he thought if he did not breathe he would die. With an almost self-destroying effort he passed this point as well and was sinking into a darker blackness when he felt the cloth being removed from his face at last.

First he breathed out the residual fouled air in his lungs, clearing his nostrils, and then, ever so slowly, despite the crying needs of his demanding body, he let a quiet trickle of air back into his lungs. Even as he did this he felt strong hands seize and lift him and carry him to the door which was opened a crack, then thrown wide so they could carry him through. There were dim night-lights in the corridor, and he slitted his eyes so they would appear closed and let his body remain completely limp despite the battering of the door-jamb as they rushed him through.

There was no one else in sight, no one to cry out to if that might have done any good. Just two men dressed completely in black with black gloves and black goggled masks over their faces that bulged out below. Two men, two rough strangers, hurrying him where?

To a waiting lift that streamed bright light when the door opened so that he closed his eyes at once. But he had recognized it, the lift from the hold up to the engine rooms that he had been in with the first engineer. What did this mean? He was jammed in, prevented from falling by the two assailants who pushed in with him so they rose silently in close, hoarse-breathing contact. While not a word was spoken. In a matter of less than a minute these two savage men had seized and bound him, theoretically rendered him unconscious and were now taking him someplace with surely no good purpose.

The answer was quick in coming. The port engine room; they were retracing his visit of that morning. Into the airlock, close the one door while the other opened—to the accompanying snakelike hissing of an exhaust valve.

There was still nothing that Washington could do. If he struggled, he would be rendered unconscious, for good this time. Though his nerves cried out for action, something to break this silence and captivity, he did nothing. His head was light by the time the inner door opened because he had breathed as deeply as he could, hyperventilating his blood, getting as much oxygen into his bloodstream as he could. Because beyond the door was the unpressurized part of the flying ship where the air was just as thin as the 12,000-foot-high atmosphere outside. Where a man simply breathed himself into gray unconsciousness and death. Was that what they had in mind? Would they leave him here to die? But why, who were they, what did they want?

They wanted to kill him. He knew that as soon as they dropped him to the cold metal of the deck and wrestled with the handles of the doorway beside him, the same one that Alec Durell had hung through in Southampton. But there he had a fall of twenty-five feet to an unwanted bath. Here there were 12,000 feet of fall to brutal death.

With a heave the door was thrown open and the 300-mile-an-hour slipstream tore through the opening, drowning out even the roar of the four great engines. It was then that Washington did what he knew he had to do.

He straightened his bent legs so they caught the nearest man behind the knees. For a brief instant the dark stranger hung there, arms flailing wildly, before vanishing through the opening into the frigid night outside.

Gus did not wait until the other had gone but was wriggling across the floor to the alarm of a fire box, struggling to his feet and butting at it with his head until he felt the glass break and slice into his skin. Turning to face the remaining man, swaying as he did so.

There is no warning to anoxia, simply a slide into unconsciousness then death. He had the single thought that the bulbous mask must contain an oxygen tank or his assailant would be falling, too. He must stay awake. Fight. Unconscious, he would be dragged to the opening and dispatched into the night like the other man.

His eyes closed and he slid slowly down and sprawled, oblivious, on the deck.

V. A PAID ASSASSIN

"A fine sunny morning, sir, bit of cloud about, but nothing to really speak of."

The steward flicked back the curtain so that a beam of molten sunlight struck into the cabin. With professional skill he pulled open the drawer on the night table and put the tray with the cup of tea upon it. At the same time he dropped the ship's newspaper onto Washington's chest so that he awoke and blinked his eyes open just as the door closed silently behind the man. He yawned as the paper drew his attention so that he glanced through the headlines. HUNDREDS FEARED DEAD IN PERUVIAN EARTHQUAKE. SHELLING REPORTED AGAIN ALONG THE RHINE. NEW YORK CITY WELCOMES CESAR CHAVEZ. The paper was prepared at the line's offices in New York, he knew that, then sent by radiocopy to the airship. The tea was strong and good, and he had slept well. Yet there was a sensation of something amiss, a stiffness on the side of his face, and he had just touched it and found a bandage there when the door was thrown open and a short, round man dressed in black and wearing a dog collar was projected through the doorway like a human cannonball, with Wing Commander Mason close behind him.

"Oh, my goodness, goodness gracious," said the spherical man, clasping and unclasping his fingers, touching the heavy crucifix he wore around his neck, then tapping the stethoscope he wore over it as though unsure whether God or Aesculapius would be of most help. "Goodness! I meant to tell the steward, dozed off, thousand pardons. Best you rest, sure of that, sleep the mender. For you, not me, of course. May I?" Even as he spoke the last he touched Gus' lower

55

eyelid with a gentle finger and pulled it down, peering inside with no less concern and awe than he would have if the owner's eternal soul had rested there.

From confusion Gus' thoughts skipped instantly to dismay, followed thereafter by a sensation of fear that sent his heart bounding and brought an instant beading of perspiration to his brow. "Then it was no dream, no nightmare." He breathed aloud. "It really happened."

The ship's commander closed the door behind him, and, once secrecy was assured, he nodded gravely.

"It did indeed, Captain Washington. Though as to what happened we cannot be sure, and it is my fondest wish that you enlighten me, if you can, as soon as possible. I can tell you only that the fire alarm sounded in the port engine room at 0011 hours Greenwich Mean Time. The first engineer, who was attending an engine in the starboard engine room at the time, responded instantly. He reports he found you alone and unconscious on the deck. Dressed as you are now, with lacerations on your face, lying directly below the fire alarm. Pieces of glass in your wounds indicate you set off the alarm with your head and this was necessitated by the fact that your ankles and wrists were secured by handcuffs. An access door in the deck nearby was open. That is all we know. The engineer, who was wearing breathing equipment, gave you his oxygen and pulled you from the deck. The Bishop of Botswana, this gentleman here, who is a physician, was called and he treated you. The manacles were cut from you, and under the bishop's direction, you were permitted to sleep. That is all we know. I hope that you will be able to tell us more."

"I can," Gus said, and his voice was hoarse. The two intent men then saw his calm, almost uncomprehending expression change to one that appeared to be that of utter despair, so profound that the priestly physician sprang forward with a cry only to be restrained by the raised hand of his patient who waved him back, at the same time drawing in a deep breath that had the hollow quality of a moan of pain, then exhaling it in what could only be a shuddering sigh.

"I remember now," he said. "I remember everything. I have killed a man."

There was absolute silence as he spoke, haltingly at first as he attempted to describe his confusion upon awakening in distress, faster and faster as he remembered the struggle in the dark, the capture, the last awful moments when another had vanished into eternity and the possibility of his own death had overwhelmed him. When he had done there were tears in the bishop's eyes, for he was a gentle man who had led a sheltered life and was a stranger to violence, while next to him the captain's eyes held no tears but instead a look of grim understanding.

"You should not blame yourself; there should be no remorse," Wing Commander Mason said, almost in the tones of a command. "The attempted crime is unspeakable. That you fought against it in self-defense is to be commended not condemned. Had I been in the same place I hope my strength of endeavor and courage would have permitted me to do the same."

"But it was I, not you, Captain. It is something I shall never forget; it is a scar I shall always carry."

"You cannot blame yourself," said the bishop, at the same time fumbling for his watch and Gus' wrist in sudden memory of his medical capacity.

"It is not a matter of blame but rather one of realization. I have done a terrible thing and the fact that it appears to be justified makes it none the less terrible."

"Yes, yes, of course," said Wing Commander Mason, a little gruffly, tugging at his beard at the same time. "But I am afraid we must carry this investigation somewhat further. Do you know who the men were—and what their possible motive might be?"

"I am as mystified as you. I have no enemies I know of."

"Did you note any distinguishing characteristics of either of them? Some tone of voice or color of hair?"

"Nothing. They were dressed in black, masked, wore gloves, did not speak but went about this business in complete silence."

"Fiends!" the bishop cried, so carried away in his emotions that he crossed himself with his stethoscope.

"But, wait, wait, the memory is there if I can only grasp it. Something, yes—a mark, blue, perhaps a tattoo of some kind.

57

One of the men, it was on his wrist, almost under my nose where he held me, revealed when his glove moved away from his jacket, on the inner side of his wrist. I can remember no details, just blue of some kind."

"Which man?" asked the captain. "The survivor or the other?"

"That I don't know. You can understand this was not my first concern."

"Indeed. Then there is a fifty-fifty chance that the man is still aboard—if he did not follow his accomplice through the opening. But by what excuse can we examine the wrists of the passengers? The crew members are well known to us but . . ." He was silent on the instant, struck by some thought that darkened his face and brought upon it a certain grimness unremarked before. When he spoke again, it was in the tones of absolute command.

"Captain Washington, please remain here quietly. The doctor will tend your needs, and I ask you to do as he directs. I will be back quite soon."

He was gone without any more explanation and before they could request one. The bishop examined Washington more thoroughly, pronounced him fit though exhausted, and recommended a soothing draught which was refused kindly but firmly.

Washington for his part lay quietly, his face set, thinking of what he had done and of what his future life might be like with a crime of this magnitude in his memory. He would have to accept it, he realized that, and learn to live with it. In the minutes that he lay there, before the door opened again, he had matured and grown measurably older so that it was almost a new individual who looked up when the captain entered for the second time. There was a bustle behind him as the first engineer, Alec, and the second officer came in, each holding firmly to the white-clad arm of a cook.

He could be nothing else, a tall and solid man all in white, chef's hat rising high on his head, sallow-skinned and neatly mustachioed, with a look of perplexity on his features. As soon as the door had been closed and the tiny cabin was crowded to suffocation with this mixed company, the captain spoke.

"This is Jacques, our cook, who has served with this ship since her commissioning and has been with Cunard ten years or more. He knows nothing of the events of last night and is concerned now only with the croissants he left to burn in the oven. But he has served me many times at table and I do recall one thing."

In a single swift motion the captain seized the cook's right arm, turning it outwards and pulling back his coat. There, on the inside of his forearm and startlingly clear against the paleness of his skin, was a blue tattoo of anchors and ropes, trellised flowers, and recumbent mermaids. Washington saw it and saw more as memory clothed the man with black instead of white, felt the strength of gloved hands again and heard the hoarseness of his breathing. Despite the bishop's attempt to prevent him he rose from the bed and stood facing the man, his face mere inches away from the other's.

"This is the one. This is the man who attempted to kill me."

For long seconds the shocked expression remained on the cook's features, a study in alarm, confusion, searching his accuser's face for meaning while Washington stared grimly and unswervingly into the other's eyes as though he were probing his soul. Then the two officers who held the man felt his arms tremble, felt his entire body begin to shake as despair seized him and replaced all else, so that instead of restraining him they found they had to support him, and when the first words broke from his lips they released a torrent of others that could not be stopped.

"Yes, I—I was there, but I was forced, not by choice, dear God as a witness not by choice. *Sacre dieu!* And remember, you fell unconscious, I could have done as I had been bid, you could not have resisted, I saved your life, left you there. Do not let them take mine, I beg of you; it was not by choice that I did any of this. . . ."

In his release it all came out, the wretched man's history since he had first set foot in England twenty years previously, as well as what his fate had been since. An illegal émigré, helped by friends to escape the grinding unemployment of Paris, friends who eventually turned out to be less than friends, none other than secret agents of the French crown. It was a simple device, commonly used, and it never failed. A request for aid that could not be refused—or he would be revealed to the English authorities and jailed, deported. Then more and more things to do while a record was kept of each, and they were illegal for the most part, until he was bound securely in a web of blackmail. Once trapped in the net he was rarely used after that, a sleeper as it is called in the filthy trade, resting like an inactivated bomb in the bosom of the country that had given him a home, ready to be sparked into ignition at any time. And then the flame. An order, a meeting, a passenger on this ship, threats and humiliations as well as the revelation that his family remaining in France would be in jeopardy if he dared refuse. He could not. The midnight meeting and the horrible events that followed. Then the final terrible moment when the agent had gone and he knew that he could not commit this crime by himself. Washington listened and understood, and it was at his instruction that the broken man was taken away—because he understood only too well. It was later, scant minutes before the flying ship began her final approach to the Narrows and a landing in New York Harbor that the captain brought Washington the final report.

"The other man is the real mystery, though it appears he was not French. A professional at this sort of thing, no papers in his luggage, no makers' marks on his clothes, an absolute blank. But he was British—everyone who spoke to him is sure of that—and had great influence or he would not be aboard this flight. All the details have been sent to Scotland Yard, and the New York Police are standing by now at the dock. It is indeed a mystery. You have no idea who your enemies might be?"

Washington sealed his last bag and dropped wearily into the chair.

"I give you my word, Captain, that until last night I had no idea I had any enemies, certainly none who could work in liaison with the French secret service and hire underground operatives." He smiled wryly. "But I know it now. I certainly know it now."

VI. IN THE LIONS' DEN

A truck had gone out of control on Third Avenue, and after caroming from one of the elevated railway pillars, mounting the curb and breaking off a water hydrant, it had turned on its side and spilled its cargo out into the street. This consisted of many bundles of varicolored cloth which had split and spread a gay bunting in all directions. The workings of chance had determined that the site of the accident could not have been better chosen for the machinations of mischief, or more ill chosen for the preserving of law and order, for the event had occurred directly in front of an Iroquois bar and grill. The occupants of the bar now poured into the street to see the fun, whooping happily through the streaming water and tearing at the bundles to see what they contained. It being a warm summer day, most of the copper-skinned men were bare above the waist, clad only in leggings and moccasins below with perhaps a headband and feather above. They pulled out great streamers of the cloth and wrapped it around themselves and laughed uproariously while the dazed truck driver hung out of the window of his cab above and shook his fist at them. The fun would have ended with this and there would have been no great mischief done if this establishment, The Laughing Water, had not been located just two doorways away from Clancy's, a drinking palace of the same order that drew its custom solely from men of Hibernian ancestry. This juxtaposition had caused much anguish to the police and the peace of the area in the past and was sure to do so in the future, and in fact promised to accomplish the same results now , in the present. The Irishmen, hearing the excitement, also came out into the street and stood making comments

61

and pointing and perhaps envying the natural exuberance of the Indians. The results were predictable and within the minute someone had been tripped, a loud name had been called, blows exchanged and a general melee resulted. The Iroquois, forced by law to check tomahawks and scalping knives at the city limits or to leave them at home if they were residents, found a ready substitute in the table knives from the grill. The Irish, equally restricted in the public display of shillelaghs and blackthorn sticks above a certain weight, found bottles and chair legs a workable substitute and joined the fray. War whoops mixed with the names of saints and the Holy Family as they clashed. There were no deaths or serious maimings since the object of the exercise was pleasure, but there were certainly broken heads and bones and at least one scalp taken, the token scalp of a bit of skin and hair. The roar of a passing el train drowned the happy cries, and when it had rumbled into oblivion, police sirens took its place. Spectators stood at a respectable distance and enjoyed the scene while barrow merchants, quick to seize the opportunity, plied the edge of the crowd selling refreshments. It was all quite enjoyable.

Ian Macintosh found it highly objectionable, not the sort of thing at all that one would ever see on the streets of Campbelltown or in Machrihanish. People who gave Highlanders a bad name for fighting and carousing ought to see the colonies first. He sniffed loudly, an act easily done since his sniffer was a monolithic prow seemingly designed for that or some more important function. It was the dominating element of Macintosh's features, nay of his entire body, for he was slight and narrow and dressed all in gray as he thought this only properly fitting, and his hair was gray while even his skin, when not exposed to the elements for too long a time, also partook of that neutral color. So it was his nose that dominated and due to its prominence and to his eager attention to details and to bookkeeping, his nickname of "Nosey" might seem to be deserved, though it was never spoken before his face, or rather before his nose.

Now he hurried by on Forty-second Street, crossing Third Avenue and sniffing one parting sniff in the direction of the melee. He pressed on through the throng, dodging skillfully even as he drew out his pocket watch and consulted it. On time, of course, on time. He was never late. Even for so distasteful a meeting as this one. What must be done must be done. He sniffed again as he pushed open the door of the Commodore Hotel, quickly before the functionary stationed there could reach it, driving him back with another sniff in case he should be seeking a gratuity for a service not performed. It was exactly two o'clock when he entered and he took some grudging pleasure from the fact that Washington was already there. They shook hands, for they had met often before, and Macintosh saw for the first time the bandages on the side of the other's face that had been turned away from him until then. Gus was aware of the object of the other's attention and spoke before the question could be asked.

"A recent development, Ian. I'll tell you in the cab."

"No cab. Sir Winthrop is sending his own car, as well he might, though it's no pleasure riding in a thing that color."

"A car need not necessarily be black," Gus said, amused, as they went up the steps to the elevated Park Avenue entrance where the elongated yellow form of the Cord Landau was waiting. Its chrome exhausts gleamed, the wire wheels shone, the chauffeur held the door for them. Once inside, with the connecting window closed, Gus explained what had happened on the airship. "And that's the all of it," he concluded. "The cook knows nothing more and the police do not know the identity of his accomplice or who might have employed him."

Macintosh snorted loudly, a striking sound in so small an enclosure, then patted his nose as though commending it for a good performance. "They know who did it and we know who did it, though proving it is another matter."

"But I'm sure *I* don't know." Gus was startled by the revelation.

"You're an engineer, Augustine, and more of an engineer than I'll ever be, but you've had your head buried in the tunnel and you've no' been watching the business end or the Stock Exchange or the Bourse."

"I don't follow."

"Then try this, if you will. If someone tries hurting you it is

63

time to see whom you might have been hurting, too. People who might have a lot of money but might see their shares slipping a wee bit. People who look to the future and see them slipping a good deal more and intend to do something about it now. People with contacts on an international level who can reach the right people in the Sûreté who are always willing to jump at a chance to make mischief for Britain. And who might they be?"

"I have no idea."

"You're being naïve, you are!" Macintosh laid his finger along his nose, which hid this digit and a good part of his hand as well, in a conspiratorial gesture. "Now I ask you, if we be under the water, who be over it?"

"Airships, but the tunnel offers them no competition. And ships upon the ocean, but . . ." His voice stopped and his features wore a startled look. Macintosh smiled a wintry smile in return.

"No names, no pack drill, and the culprits will be hard to find I warrant. But a command may be spoken, half in jest perhaps—and I ask you to remember Thomas Becket!—an order relayed, an order given, an ambitious man, money changes hands. I shall not spell it out, but I can and do suggest that you beware in the future."

The car stopped then before one of the taller buildings in Wall Street and they emerged with Gus in a speculative state of mind. There was more to constructing a tunnel than digging a hole he realized, and apparently assassins could now be assumed to be an occupational hazard. Along with boards of directors. But he was prepared for the latter at least, had been preparing for this day for the past week, bolstering his facts, pinning down his figures. Taking a chance, a leap into the darkness that had been troubling him ever since he had first realized what must be done. His career rested upon the outcome of today's meeting and rightly enough it concerned him deeply. But since the previous night when he had been face to face with a far more literal and final leap into the darkness, his will had been strengthened. What must be done must be done—and he would do it.

Sir Winthrop he knew, and shook his hand, and was introduced to the other members of the board whom he was acquainted with only by name and reputation. **Self-made** men all of them, solid and sure of themselves, twenty-one different individuals who blended into one as he looked. One man, one body of men, whom he had to convince. As he seated himself at the place reserved for him at the long table, he realized that the meeting had been in session for some time if the state of the ashtrays was any indication; since these men were experienced marksmen the spittoons showed no such evidence. This was clear proof that he had been deliberately invited to arrive after the proposals regarding his new status had been put before the board. There were no echoes of discussion in the heavy drapes that framed the windows or in the rich cigar fragrance of the air, but some hint of differences of opinion could be detected in the rigid scowls and set faces of a few of the board members. Obviously the unanimity of opinion did not exist here as it did on the board in London; but Gus had expected this. He knew the state of mind of his fellow colonials and had marshaled his facts to override any objections.

"Gentlemen of the board," said Sir Winthrop, "we have been discussing one matter for some time now, that is the possibility of my stepping down as chairman of this board to be replaced by Captain Washington, who will also be in charge of the engineering of the tunnel here. This change has been forced upon us by the disastrous state of the finances of the entire operation, finances that must be mended if we are to have any operation at all. It was decided to postpone a vote upon this matter until the captain could be spoken to and interrogated. He is here. Ah, I see Mr. Stratton wishes to begin."

Mr. Stratton's lean figure rose from its chair like a vulture ascending, a jointed collection of black suiting and white skin with darkset eyes and pointed accusing finger, an upsetting apparition at any time and even more so now as he rattled with anger.

"No good, no good at all, we can't have our firm represented by a man with the name of Washington, no not at all. As soon have Judas Iscariot as board chairman, or Pontius Pilate, or Guy Fawkes. . . ."

"Stratton, would you kindly confine yourself to the matter

at hand and reserve the historical lecture for another time."

The speaker of these quiet but acidulous words lolled at ease in his chair, a short and fat roly-poly sort of man with a great white beard that flowed over his chest, a great black cigar that stuck up out of his mouth like a flagstaff—and a cold, penetrating eye that belied any impression of laxity or softness that the exterior might suggest.

"You'll hear me out, Gould, and stay silent. There are some things that cannot be forgotten—"

"There are some things that are better off forgotten," came the interruption again. "It is almost two hundred years now and you are still trying to fight the rebellion over again. Enough, I say. Your ancestors were Tories, very nice for them; they picked the winning side. If they had lost we would be calling them traitors now and maybe George Washington would have had them shot the way they squeezed poor old German George to shoot him. Maybe you got guilt feelings about that, huh? Which is why you keep scratching all the time at this same itch. For the record I got ancestors, too, and one of them was involved, a Haym Solomon, poor shlub lost everything he had financing the revolution and ended up selling pickles out of a barrel on the East Side. Does this bother me? Not a bit. I vote the straight Tory ticket now because that is the party of the big money and I got big money. Let bygones be bygones."

"Then you were as unlucky in your choice of ancestors as Washington was," Stratton snapped back, bristling and crackling with anger and shooting his cuffs in a manner which suggested that he wished there were some real shooting of certain people involved. "I wouldn't brag about it if I were you. In any case the public at large is not aware of your indecorous lineage, whereas the name Washington has an ineradicable taint. The American public will rise in arms against anything connected with a name so odious."

"Yore full of hogwash, Henry," a leathery Texas voice drawled out from a large man far down the table who wore a wide-brimmed hat, despite the fact the others were all bareheaded. "In the West we have a hard job rememberin' where New England is much less the details of all your

Yankee feudin'. If this engineer feller can sell the stock fer us, I say hire him and be done with it."

"Me, too," a deep voice boomed in answer from a copper-skinned individual even farther along the board. "All that the Indians know is that all white men are no good. Too many of us were shot up before the Peace of 1860. If oil hadn't been discovered on Cherokee lands, I wouldn't be sitting here now. I say hire him."

There was more spirited crosstalk after this that was finally hammered into silence by the chairman's gavel. He nodded to Gus who rose and faced them all.

"What Mr. Stratton has to say is very important. If the name of Washington will do injury to the tunnel, this fact must be taken into consideration, and if true I will withdraw at once from the position that is under discussion. But I feel, as others here apparently do as well, that old hatreds are best forgotten in the new era. Since the original thirteen states attempted to form their own government and failed, this country has grown until now it numbers thirty-one states and the California Territory. Living in these states are the various Indian tribes who care little, as Chief Sunflower has told you, of our ancient squabbles. Also in these states are refugees from the Baltic wars, Jewish refugees from the Russian pogroms, Dutch refugees from the Dike disaster, Swedish refugees from the Danish occupation, people from many different states and nations who also do not care about these same ancient squabbles. I say that they will be far more interested in the percentage of return upon their investment than they will in my grandfather's name. It is unimportant and not relevant at this time. What is important is the plan I have conceived that will attract investors, and it is my wish that you hear this plan before voting upon my qualifications for the position. You will be buying a pig in a poke if you do anything different. Let me tell you what I want to do, then, if you agree that my plans have merit, vote for them and not the individual who proposes them. If you think them bad, then I am not the one you want and I will return to my tunnel in England and no more will be said on the subject."

"Now that's what I call plain talk. Let's hear the boy out."

There were cries of agreement at this proposal, and Stratton's rattle of defiance was lost in the general approval. Gus nodded and opened his case and drew out the mass of papers he had so carefully prepared.

"Gentlemen, my only aim is to save the tunnel and this is the plan that I put before you. This is all I have come to do. If I can help by being a figurehead, then I shall climb up on the bowsprit of the corporate ship and suspend myself from it. I am an engineer. My fondest ambition is to be part of the building of the transatlantic tunnel. The British board of directors feels that I can aid most by being put in charge of the American end of the tunnel, so that the American public will see that this is an American enterprise as well. I do not wish to replace Mr. Macintosh but to aid him, so that we can pull in a double harness. I hope he will remain as my first assistant in all matters of construction and my equal, if not my superior, in the matter of supplies and logistics, for he is an expert in these matters." A buglelike sniff announced that this statement was not amiss in at least one quarter.

"In relation to this board let my position be literally that of a figurehead—though I would suggest this intelligence be kept within this room. I am no financier and my hope is that Sir Winthrop will continue in his original function *pro tem* until the time arrives when he can fulfill it in the public eye as well. I wish to build this tunnel and build it well, and build it quickly so that a fair profit can be returned on investments. That is my prime function. Secondly, I must publicize this construction in such a manner that investors will flock to our banner and thrust dollars upon us in ever-growing sums."

"Hear, hear!" someone called out while another said, "And how will that be done?"

"In the following manner. We shall abandon the present technique of construction and proceed in a different, cheaper, faster way that will have a broader base in the economy. Which stirring up of the economy, I believe, was one of the motivating factors in the first place."

"Does Sir Isambard know of this?" Macintosh called out, his face flushed, the twin dark barrels of his nostrils aimed like mighty guns.

"To be very frank—he does not. Though we have discussed it many times in the past. His decision has been to continue the present slip-casting technique until it proves impracticable, if ever, and only then to consider different methods of construction. I thought him wrong, but as long as I was subordinate there was nothing I could do. Now that I hope to assume what might be called an independent command I am exercising my judgment to make a change to a more modern, a more American technique, to—"

"To stab him in the back!"

"Nothing of the sort."

"Let him talk, Scotty," the Texan called out. "He's makin' sense so far."

He had their attention and at least the sympathy of some. Now if he could only convince them. There was absolute silence as Washington took a blueprint from his case and held it up.

"This is what we are doing now, building the tunnel by slip casting, what has been called the most modern technique. As the tunneling shield is pushed ahead and ground removed, this great metal tube is pushed along behind it. Reinforcing rods are put in place outside the tube and concrete is pumped in. The concrete sets, the tube is advanced again, and the end result is a continuous tunnel that is cast in place. The shield moves ahead at a varying rate but never averaging more than thirty feet a day. Very impressive. Until you consider the width of the Atlantic. If this rate continues steadily—and we have no guarantee that it will, plus plenty of suspicion it will not—we will reach the midpoint in the Atlantic at the same time, hopefully, as the British tunnel arrives, in something in the neighborhood of one hundred and five thousand days. That, gentlemen, is a bit over two hundred years."

Rightly enough there was a murmur of dismay over this and some quick calculations on the scratch pads.

"The figure is a disheartening one, I agree, and most investors care for a quicker return, but happily it is not the final one. What I suggest is that we replace the technique we are now using which will speed the process greatly, while at the same time giving a great lift to the American economy in all spheres; shipbuilding, steel, engineering, and many more. And it will reduce the time needed for construction as well.

"Reduce it to about ten years' time."

Not surprisingly, there was instant consternation over this statement as well as excitement, and one man's voice rose above the roar and spoke for them all.

"How, I want to know, just tell me how!"

The hubbub died away as Washington took a drawing from his case and unfolded it and held it up for their inspection.

"This is how. You will note that this is a section of tunnel some ninety feet in length and constructed of reinforced concrete. It contains two rail tunnels, side by side, and a smaller service tunnel below. This is what the tunnel we are driving now looks like. The smaller tunnel is known as an adit and is driven first. In this manner we can test the rock and soil that we shall be digging through and know what problems face the larger tunnels. These tunnels are driven side by side and are connected at intervals by cross chambers. All in all a complex and technical manner to tunnel and we should be very happy with the thirty feet a day we have been averaging. Except for the fact that we have thousands of miles to go. Therefore I suggest what may appear to be novel and untried, but let me assure you that this technique has been tried and found true in this country, in the tunnels under Delaware Bay and the Mississippi River and in other parts of the world such as Hong Kong Harbor. The technique is this: The tunnel is preformed and precast and built in sections ashore—then floated to the site and sunk. Built under the best conditions possible, tested for defects, left to cure and set, and only then allowed to become a part of the tunnel.

"Can you gentlemen visualize what this will mean? All along the Atlantic seaboard and in the Gulf of Mexico shipyards and newly constructed facilities will be prefabricating the sections—even in the Great Lakes and on the St. Lawrence River the yards will be busy. Vast amounts of steel and concrete will be needed almost at once—it goes without saying that those who have invested in steel and concrete stand to make a good deal of money. Contracts will be let to anyone who can prove he will supply the goods. The economy of this nation cannot help but be vitalized by an economic injection of such magnitude. The tunnel will be built, and in the building thereof this great country of ours will be built anew!"

There were cheers at that, for Gus had fired them with his own enthusiasm and they believed him. There was even more scribbling on pads and quick looks at the *Wall Street Journal* to see what the condition of steel and concrete stocks were; already some of the men were using their pocket telegraphs to get in touch with their brokers. A feeling of new life had swept the room and there were very few, one individual in particular, who did not share in the overriding enthusiasm. When the noise had died down, Macintosh spoke.

"Sir Isambard must be notified of this suggestion. Nothing can be done without his approval."

Loud catcalls mixed with boos greeted this suggestion, and it was Sir Winthrop who spoke to the point.

"I do not think that will be necessary. The financing of the tunnel is in trouble or this special meeting would not have been held, and Captain Washington would not have been sent here in his present capacity. He has a free hand from London, you must remember that, he has a free hand. If the financial obligations are not met on this side of the Atlantic then there will be no tunnel at all. If this change in technique will assure success, and I have no reason to believe differently, then we must adopt it. Nothing else is possible."

There were questions then, all of them answered with precision and facts, as well as a small amount of opposition mostly in the form of the gentleman from New England.

"Mark my words—it will be a disaster. A name like Washington can only bring the worst results—"

He was shouted into silence, and there was at least one cry of "Take his scalp!" which would be singularly difficult since the hair that presumably once had resided there had long vanished, but the utterance of which made him clap his hand to his head and sit down with great alacrity so that this voice of dissent from the general opinion was silenced and there were no others to occupy its place. A verbal vote was taken

71

and carried with a good deal of cheering and only when silence reigned again did Macintosh stand, shaking with anger, and address his closing remarks to them all.

"Then so be it, I'll not argue. But I consider this small repayment to the great man who conceived and designed this tunnel." He stabbed out a damning finger. "A man who took you into his home, Augustine Washington, to whose daughter I do believe you are engaged. Have you ever thought what effect this decision will have on that young lady?"

The room was silent at this for, in his enthusiasm to defend his employer and friend, Macintosh had overstepped the bounds of polite society and had entered the distasteful areas of personalities and abuse. He must have realized this even as the words left his mouth because he blanched a grayer gray and started to sit, then rose again as Washington turned to face him. The American's features were set and firm, but an observant eye would have noticed how all the tendons and veins rose up from the back of his hands and how bloodless his knuckles were where he clenched them. He spoke.

"I am glad this was mentioned, since it is sure to be questioned by someone else at some later date. Firstly, I still admire and respect Sir Isambard as my mentor and employer and have nothing but the greatest regard for him. In his sagacity he bids us wait to use this new tunneling technique and we would wait had we but the time and the money. We do not. So we will proceed with a plan that has his approval at least in theory if not in application at the present time. I wish him nothing but goodwill and even understand his attitude toward me. He who stands alone on Olympus does not wish to make room for others. And he does stand alone as the engineer and builder of our age. When my new role in the American developments was voted upon in London, he felt he had been done a personal injury and I can understand that, too. He has forbidden me his house, and I do not blame him in any way because according to his lights he is correct. He has also insisted that the engagement between myself and his daughter be terminated, and this has been done. I will not discuss my personal feelings with you gentlemen other than to say I wish it were not so. But it is. In one sense it is a good thing because it frees me to make the correct decision, for the tunnel if not for myself.

"The money shall be raised and the tunnel shall be built in the manner I have outlined."

End of the First Book

Book the Second

Under the Sea

I. AN UNUSUAL JOURNEY

The silence in the little cabin was almost absolute and were it not for the constructions and devices of man it would have been absolute, for here at thirty fathoms of depth in the Atlantic there was no sound. On the ocean's surface above, the waves might crash and roar and ships' foghorns moan as the vessels groped their way through the almost constant fogs of the Grand Banks off Newfoundland, and nearer the surface pelagic life made its own moans as it was consumed; the shrimp clicked, the dolphin beeped, the fish burbled. Not so at the level where the tiny submarine sped; here was the eternal quiet of the deep. Stillness outside and almost as still within. There was only the distant hum of the electric motors that drove them through the water, the sibilant whisper of the air vents and, surprisingly, the loudest, the tack-tack-tack of the jackdaw clock fixed to the bulkhead above the pilot. There had been no conversation for some minutes and in that vacuum the clock sounded the louder. The pilot saw his passenger's glance move to it and he smiled.

"You'll be noticing the clock then, Captain," said he, not without a certain amount of pride.

"I do indeed," said Washington, failing to add that it was impossible not to notice the obtruding thing. "I assume it is an original?"

"Not only an original, but it is close on being the original, one of the very first ones made, that's what it is. My grandfather it was who built the first jackdaw clock after seeing one of them things from the Black Forest when he was in a hock shop on O'Connell Street. Cuckoo clock it was, he said, and it fascinated him, what with him being a clockmaker himself and all that. When he came home to Cashel, he tried to build one, but not being overfond of cuckoos himself, great ugly things laying eggs in others' nests and such incivility, he put in a jackdaw and a bit of ruined tower, that being where jackdaws are found in any case and there it was. He made first one and then another and they caught on with the English tourists out to look at the Castle and the Rock, and before you could say Brian O'Lynn an entire new industry was founded and to this day you'll see a statue of him in the square there in Cashel."

As though to add emphasis to this panegyric the clock struck the hour and the jackdaw emerged through the portal of the ruined abbey and hoarsely shouted "Cawr, cawr" before retreating.

"Is it two already?" asked Washington, looking at his watch which was in rough agreement with the jackdaw who had retired to his dark cell for another hour. "Are we going as fast as we can?"

"Full revs, Captain, *Nautilus* is doing her best." The pilot pushed the speed lever harder against its stop as though to prove his point. "In any case there's the site now."

O'Toole turned off the outside lights so they could see farther through the darkness of the sea. Above them there was a filtered greenness that vanished as the depth increased so that below there was only unrelieved blackness. Yet when the glow of the beams had died away, something could be seen down there in abyss, light where only night had ruled since the world was born. One light was visible, then another and another until a cluster of submerged stars greeted them as they dropped lower, welcoming them to a hive of industry alien to the ancient peace of the ocean floor.

First of all, the eye was captured by a hulking, squat, ugly, alien, angular, boomed, buttressed, and barbicaned machine that clutched the ocean floor. It had the girder and rivet look of a sturdy bridge, for well over ninety-five percent of its construction was open to the ocean, at a pressure equilibrium with the sea around it. The frame was open and the reaching arms were open, while the tractor treads were jointed plates that ran on sturdy cast-iron wheels. It took a keen eye to note the swollen bulges behind the treads that contained the electric motors to power them, though the rotund shape of the nuclear reactor, swung like a melon behind the great machine, was certainly easy enough to see. Other motors in pods turned the gear wheels and cables while the most important pod of all made a rounded excrescence on the front of the entire structure. This was the control room and living quarters of the crew, pressurized, comfortable, and habitable, and so self-contained that the men could live here for months on end without returning to the world above the waves that was their natural habitat. Yet so large was the great supporting device that even these stately quarters were no larger in proportion than an egg would be balanced on the handlebars of a bicycle, which, in some ways, the structure did resemble.

This hulking machine, entitled the Challenger Mark IV Dredger by its manufacturers, was nonetheless called Creepy by all who came into contact with it, undoubtedly because of its maximum speed of about one mile an hour. Creepy was neither creeping nor operating at the present time which was all for the best since otherwise vision would have been completely impossible, for while at work it threw up an obscuring cloud in the water denser than the finest inky defense of the largest squid alive. Its booms would then swing out and the rotating cutters each as large as an omnibus would crash into the ocean floor, while about them com-pressed streams of water tore at the silt and sand deposits of this bed. Under the attack of the water and the cutting blades the eternal floor of the ocean would be stirred and lifted—in-to the mouths of suction dredgers that sucked at this slurry, raised and carried it far to the side where it was spewed forth in a growing mound. All of this agitation raised a cloud of fine particles in the water that completely obscured vision and was penetrable only by the additional application of scientific knowledge. Sound waves will travel through water, opaque or no, and the returned echoes of the sonar scanner built up a picture on the screen of events ahead in the newly dug trench. But Creepy's work was done for the moment, its motors silent, its digging apparatus raised when it had backed away from the new trench.

Other machines now took their place upon the ocean floor. There was an ugly device with a funnel-like proboscis that spat gravel into the ditch, but this had finished as well and also backed away and the silt raised by its disturbance quickly settled. Now the final work had begun, the reason for all this subaqueous excavation. Floating downwards toward the newly dug trench and the bed of gravel on which it was to rest was the ponderous and massive form of a preformed tunnel section. Tons of concrete and steel reinforcing rods had gone into the construction of this hundred-foot section, while coat after coat of resistant epoxies covered it on the outside. Preformed and prestressed, it awaited only a safe arrival to continue the ever-lengthening tunnel. Thick cables rose from the embedded rings to the even larger flotation tank that rode above it, for it had no buoyancy of its own. The tubes that would be the operating part of the tunnel were open to the sea at both ends. Massive and unyielding, it hung there, now drifting forward slowly under the buzzing pressure of four small submarines, sister vessels to the one that Washington was riding in. They exchanged signals, stopping and starting, then drifting sideways, until they were over the correct spot in the trench. Then water was admitted to the ballast tanks of the float so it dropped down slowly, setting the structure to rest on its prepared bed. With massive precision the self-aligning joint between the sections performed its function so that when the new section came to rest it was joined to and continuous with the last. The subs buzzed down and the manipulating apparatus on their bows clamped hydraulic jacks over the flanges and squeezed slowly to make the two as one. Only when the rubber seals had been collapsed as far as their stops did they halt and hold fast while the locking plates were fixed in place. On the bottom other crawling machines were already waiting to put the sealing forms around the junction so the special tremie, underwater setting concrete, could be poured around the ends to join them indivisibly.

All was in order, everything as it should be, the machines below going about their tasks as industriously as ants around a nest. Yet this very orderliness was what drew Gus' thoughts to the object off to one side, the broken thing, the near catastrophe that for a brief while had threatened the entire project.

A tunnel section. Humped and crushed with one end buried deep in the silt of the ocean's floor.

Had it been only twenty-four hours since the accident? One day. No more. Men now alive would never forget the moments when the supporting cable broke and the section had started its tumbling fall toward the tunnel and Creepy close below it. One submarine, one man, had been at the right spot at the right time and had done what needed to be done. One tiny machine, propeller spinning, had stayed in position, pushing with all its power so that the fall had shifted from a straight line and had moved ever so slightly to one side, enough to clear the tunnel and the machines below. But machine and man had paid the price for so boldly pitting themselves against the mass of that construction, for when the tunnel section had struck and broken, it had risen up like an avenging hammer and struck the mote that presumed to fight against it. One man had died; many had been saved. The name of Aloysius O'Brian would be inscribed on the slate of honor. The first death and as honorable a one as a man could want, if a man could be said to want death at all. Washington breathed heavily at the thought, because there would be other deaths, many deaths, before this tunnel was completed. The pilot saw the direction of his passenger's gaze and read his thoughts as easily as though they had been spoken aloud.

"And a good man, Aloysius was, even if he came from Waterford. The Irish make good submariners and no empty boast is that, and if ever anyone should doubt that, you just tell them about himself out there with a thousand-ton tombstone and what he did. But don't fret yourself, Captain. The other section is on the way, the replacement for that one, hours away but moving steadily, the thing will be done."

"May it be the truth, O'Toole, the very truth."

The next section had already appeared and was visible in the lights below, and Gus knew that the final ones were waiting out there in the darkness, with the ultimate one coming as fast as the tugs could pull. Under his directions the sub moved along the length of the trench the short distance to the two completed sections of tunnel that projected from the caisson that would some day be the Grand Banks Station. The ocean here was no more than eleven fathoms deep, which made the dumping of the rubble for the station that much easier. The artificial island rose up to the surface before them, an island growing all the time as barge after barge of stone and sand was added to it. Gus looked at his watch and pointed ahead.

"Take us up," he ordered.

A floating dock was secured here and they rose next to it and there was the thud of the magnetic grapple striking the hull as they were hauled into position. O'Toole worked the controls that opened the hatches above and the fresh, damp ocean air struck moistly against Gus' face as he climbed to the deck. The sun had set unremarked while he had been below the ocean's surface, and the fog, temporarily held at bay by the warming rays, was returning in all haste as though to make up for time lost. Streamers of it rolled across the dock, bearing with them a sudden chill in the northern September evening. A ladder had been lowered to the submarine and Gus climbed toward the sailor waiting above who saluted him as he stepped from it.

"Captain's compliments, sir, and he says the ship is waiting and we'll cast off as soon as you're aboard."

Gus followed the man, yawning as he did, for it had been a long day, beginning well before dawn, and it was the latest of an endless series of similar days stretching into the past longer than he could remember. When he looked in the mirror to shave, he was sometimes startled at the stranger who looked back at him, a man with an unhealthy pallor from being too long away from the sun, dark-burned circles under the eyes from being too often away from his bed, touches of gray around the temples from too much responsibility too long borne. But no regrets ever, for what he was doing was worth doing, the game worth the candle. His only regret even now was that, although he had a full night ahead of him when he could sleep, this night would be spent aboard H.M.S. *Boadicea* known affectionately to her crew as Old Bonebreaker for the quality of her passage over troubled waters. She was a hovercraft, the newest addition to the Royal American Coast Guard, capable of fifty knots over even the most towering seas, or sand or swamp or solid ground for that matter, the revenue agent's delight, the smuggler's dread; at top speed she rode like a springless lorry on a washboard road so was not the vessel of choice when one wanted a good night's sleep. But speed was the point of this trip, not sleep, and speed was what this unusual vehicle could certainly guarantee. Captain Stokes himself was waiting at the top of the gangplank, and his welcoming smile was sincere as he shook Washington's hand.

"A pleasure to have you aboard, Captain Washington," was spoken quietly. "Cast off those lines" exploded out like the shell from a gun toward the ratings on deck. "Reports say a moderate swell, so we should be able to maintain fifty-five knots for most of the night. If the seas stay that smooth, our ETA at Bridgehampton will be dawn. Reporter chap coming along for the ride, no way to stop him, hope you don't mind."

"Not at all, Captain. Publicity has been the making of this tunnel, so when the press wants to see me I am available."

The reporter stood up when they entered the officers' mess, a sturdy, sandy man in a checked suit, wearing a bowler, the traditional hat of all newsmen. He was one of the new breed of electronic reporters, the recording equipment slung on his back like a pack, with the microphone peeping over one shoulder, the lens of the camera over the other. "Biamonte of the New York *Times*, Captain Washington. And I'm pool man, too, drawer of the lucky straw, since only one reporter could come on this voyage, so I'm AP, UP, Reuters, *Daily News*, the lot. I have a few questions—"

"Which I will be more than happy to answer in a few moments. But I have never been aboard a hovercraft before, and I would like to watch her when she pulls out."

Scarcely a second was being wasted on the departure. The two great propellers mounted on towers in the stern were already beginning to turn over as the lines that secured *Boadicea* to the dock were being cast off. The thrust propellers for the surface effect must have been turned on at the same time for the great craft shifted and stirred, then, strangest sensation of all, began to lift straight up into the air. Higher and higher—six, eight, ten feet—it lifted until it was literally riding on a cushion of air and had no contact with the water at all. The thrust propellers were now just silvery disks, disks that could pivot back or forth on top of their mounts, and swing about they did until they faced crosswise rather than fore and aft and under their pressure the craft floated easily away from the dock. They turned again, thrusting now at full speed and bit by bit the modern *Boadicea* became a lady conqueror of the waves, riding up and over them, faster and faster, rushing south into the night. But the hammering and shaking increased as she did, so that the plates rattled in the racks and the charts in their cupboards and Gus gratefully sought the softening comfort of the sofa. Biamonte sat across from him and touched buttons on his hand controller.

"Are we going to win, Captain Washington, that is the question that is on everyone's lips today? Shall we win?"

"It has never been a question of winning or losing. Circumstances were almost completely governed by chance so that the American section of tunnel is reaching completion to the shelf station just about the same time as the English section to their station on the Great Sole Bank. There never was a race. The situations are different, even the distances involved are different."

"They certainly are and that is what makes this race that you won't call a race so exciting. The American tunnel is three times as long as the English. . . ."

"Not quite three times."

"But still a good deal longer, you'll have to admit, and to build our tunnel in the same length of time as theirs is in itself a victory and a source of pride to all Americans. It will be an even greater victory if you can make a trip through the entire length of the American tunnel and then reach London in time to be aboard the first train to pass through the English tunnel. That train will be leaving Paddington Station in less than thirty hours. Do you still think you will be aboard it?"

"I have every expectation."

The hovercraft had reached its maximum speed now and was hammering along like a demented railway carriage, leaping from wave to wave. Biamonte swallowed and loosened his collar as a fine beading of perspiration appeared on his brow; for those of delicate tummies the hovercraft is not a recommended form of transportation. But, sick or well, he was still a reporter and he pressed on.

"Does not the fact that one segment of the tunnel was destroyed interfere with your chances of winning?"

"I wish you would not refer to winning or losing since I feel it does not apply. In answer to your question, no, it has not altered the situation appreciably. Extra sections were constructed, reserve sections, in case faults developed in any of the others during construction. The final section is on its way now and will be placed during the night."

"Would you care to comment upon the fact that Mr. J. E. Hoover, of the Long Island region branch of the Colonial Bureau of Investigation, thinks that sabotage may be involved with the broken cable and that he has a man in custody?"

"I have no comment since I know no more about it than you do."

Gus kept all emotion from his voice, giving no hint that this was not the first case of attempted sabotage to the project. The reporter was now turning an interesting shade of green and noticed nothing. Yet he persevered with his questions despite a growing glassiness of the eye and a certain hoarseness of voice.

"Since the accident the bookmakers' odds have fallen from five to three in your favor to even money. Does the immense amounts wagered upon your reaching London in time bother you at all?"

"Not in the slightest. Gambling is not one of my vices."

"Would you tell me what your vices are?"

"Not answering that sort of question is one of them."

They both smiled at this light exchange, though Biamonte's smile had a certain fixed or frozen quality. He definitely was green now and had some small difficulty speaking as *Boadicea* charged the briny hills with undiminished energy.

"More seriously then . . . would you explain . . . the importance of these stations . . . in the ocean . . . for the tunnel."

"Certainly. If you had before you a three-dimensional map of the world with all the waters of the oceans stripped away, you would see that the seas bordering the British Isles and North America are quite shallow, relatively speaking. Here we have the continental shelf, shoal water, stretching along our coast up to Canada and out past the island of Newfoundland to the Grand Banks that border the abyssal plain. An underwater cliff begins here, steep, sharp, and deep, dropping more abruptly than any mountain range on earth. You saw the artificial island that is the beginning of the Grand Banks Station. It stands in sixty-six feet of water. Beyond this the bottom drops sharply down to over fifteen thousand feet, three miles in depth. The British Point Two Hundred in the Great Sole Bank stands in forty-two feet of water, also at the edge of a three-mile drop. These two stations mark the limits of our shallow water operations, and beyond them we will have to use different types of tunnels and different types of trains. Therefore train junctions must be built as well as. . . ."

He did not finish because the reporter was no longer there. With a strangled gasp he had clutched at his mouth and rushed from the room. It was something of a wonder to Gus, who had a cast-iron constitution when it came to things of this sort, why people behaved like this, though he knew some did. But the interruption was timely since it gave him an opportunity to get some rest. He found the captain on the bridge, and after a brief but interesting talk concerning the technologies of this new-fangled craft, the captain offered his own quarters for the use of his visitor. The bed was most comfortable, and Gus fell at once into a deep though not undisturbed sleep. Complete relaxation was not possible and his eyes were already open when the messboy brought in a cuplike container with a spout in its top.

"Coffee, sir, fresh from the thermos, sugar and cream like I hope you like. Just suck on the top there, splash-proof valve, easy enough to work once you catch on."

It was, and the coffee was good. After a wash and a quick shave Gus felt immensely better as he climbed back to the bridge. Astern, the sea was washed with golden light as dawn approached, while ahead dark night still reigned, though the stars were going and the low outline of Long Island could be clearly seen. The lighthouse on Montauk Point flashed welcome and within a few minutes its form could be clearly seen against the lightening sky. The captain, who had not quit his bridge the entire night, bid Washington a good morning then passed him a piece of paper.

"This was received by radio a few minutes ago." Gus opened it and read.

CAPT. G. WASHINGTON ABOARD H.M.S. BOADICEA. FINAL SECTION INSTALLED SEALING CONTINUED AS PLANNED. EOC EIGHT FEET GOWAN WILL UNIFY ALL IN THE GREEN. SAPPER

"I am afraid the radio operator was quite mystified," said Captain Stokes. "But he had the message repeated and says this is correct."

"It certainly is, and the news could not be better. All of the sections of the tunnel are in place and are being sealed together for a water-tight bond. As you undoubtedly know, other sections of the tunnel were extended back from the Grand Banks Station to meet the ones coming the other way. Surveying is not easy on the ocean floor, plus the fact that we wanted some leeway when the two tunnels met. While we can manufacture sections of tunnel underwater, we cannot shorten sections already fabricated. Our error of closure was eight feet, almost exactly what we estimated it would be. Right now mud is being poured between the ends and this will be stabilized with the Gowan units; they will freeze it solid with liquid nitrogen so we can bore through. Everything is going as planned."

Gus had not realized that the others on the bridge, the steersman, sailors, and officers, all of them, had been listening as he spoke, but he was made aware of this as a cheer broke out from them.

"Silence!" the captain roared. "You act like a herd of raw boots, not seamen." Yet he was smiling as he said it, for he shared their enthusiasm. "You are destroying the morale of my ship, Captain Washington, but just this once I do not mind. Though we are Royal Coast Guard and as loyal to the Queen as any others, we are still Americans. What you have done, are doing, with your tunnel, has done more to unify us and remind us of our American heritage than anything I can remember. This is a great day and we are behind you one hundred percent."

Gus seized his hand, firmly. "I shall never forget those words, Captain, for they mean more to me than any prizes or awards. What I do I do for this country, to unite it. I ask no more."

Then they were entering the outer harbor at Bridgehampton, slowing so the spray no longer rose in great sheets around them. This sleepy little town near the tip of Long Island had changed radically in the years since the tunnel had begun, for here was the American terminus of the great project. A few white frame houses of the original inhabitants remained along the shore, but most had been swallowed in the docks, ramps, boatworks, assembly plants, storehouses, marshaling yards, offices, barracks, buildings, boom and bustle that had overwhelmed the town. *Boadicea* pointed toward the beach and slid over the surf and up onto the sand where it finally settled to rest. As soon as the storm of blowing particles had ceased, a police car raced across the hard-packed surface and slid to a stop. The driver opened the door and saluted as Washington came down the ramp.

"I was told to meet you, sir. The special train is waiting."

As indeed it was, as well as a cheering crowd of early risers, or rather nonrisers and nonsleepers, most of whom must have spent the coolish night here in vigil, warming themselves around now cold bonfires, rousing up to listen to every word of Washington's progress as it was passed down from the tunnel headquarters. They were on his side and he was their hero so the general joy and noise rose to a fever pitch when he appeared, while the mob seethed and churned like a soup pot on the boil as everyone wanted to get closer at the same time. A platform had been erected, draped with flags and bunting, where a red-faced band sat and trumpeted loud but unheard music that was drowned completely by the thunderous ovation. Everyone there wanted to greet Washington, shake his hand, touch his clothing, have some contact with this man upon this day. The police could not have prevented them, but a gang of navvies could and did, and they surrounded him with the solidness of their bodies and boots and tramped a path toward the waiting train. On the way they passed the stand which Washington mounted, to shake hands quickly with the silk-hatted dignitaries there and to wave to the crowd. They cheered even more loudly, then fell almost silent so his words reached them all.

"Thank you. This is America's day. I'm going now."

Concise but correct and then he was on his way again to the train where a strong bronze hand reached down to half lift him into the single coach behind the electric engine. No sooner had his feet touched the step than the train began to move, picking up speed quickly, rattling through the points and rushing at the black opening framed by the proud words, *Transatlantic Tunnel.*

Gus had no sooner seated himself than that same elevating bronze hand became a bearing hand and produced a bottle of beer which it presented, open and frothing, to him. Since beef and beer are the lifeblood of the navvies, he had long since accustomed himself to this diet, at any hour of the day and night, so that he now seized the bottle as though he normally broke his fast with this malt beverage, as indeed he had many times, and raised it to his lips. The owner of this same bronze hand had another bottle ready which he also lifted and half drained at a swallow, then sighed with pleasure.

Sapper Cornplanter, of the Oneida tribe of the Iroquois Nation, head ganger of the tunnel, loyal friend. He was close to seven feet of copper-skinned bone and sinew and muscle, black-haired, black of eye, slow to anger but when angry a juggernaut of justice with fists the size of Virginia hams and hard as granite. A gold circlet with an elk's tooth pendant from it hung from his right ear and he twisted it between his fingers now as he thought, as was his habit when deep concentration was needed. The twisted elk's tooth by some internal magic twisted up his thoughts into a workable bundle and when they were nicely tightened and manageable he produced the result.

"You're cutting this whole operation mighty fine, Captain."

"A conclusion I had reached independently, Sapper. Do you have any reason to think that I won't make it?"

"Nothing—except the fact that you have no leeway, no fat in the schedule at all in case of the unforeseen and I might remind you that the unforeseen is something tunnelers always have to take into consideration. The tunnel sections are all in place and the tremie seals between the joints poured, everything is going as well as might be expected. The last five tunnel sections are still filled with water since we need some hours for the joints to seal. On your orders. Want me to phone ahead and have them drained?"

"Absolutely not, since we need as much time as possible for the setting. Just make sure the equipment is ready so we can get right at it. Now what about my connection at the station?"

"The RAF helithopter is already there, fueled and standing by. As well as the Wellington in Gander. They will get you through just as long as the Great Spirit showers his blessings, but there is a chance that He will shower more than blessings. There is a weather low out in the Atlantic, force nine winds and snow, moving in the direction of Newfoundland, and it looks like heap big trouble."

"May I get there first!"

"I'll drink to that." And he was as good as his word, producing two more bottles of Sitting Bull beer from the case beneath his seat.

With ever-increasing speed the train drove deeper into that black tunnel under the Atlantic, retracing the course beneath the sea that the hove craft had so recently taken above it. But here, far away from the weather and the irregularities of wind and wave, over a roadbed made smooth by the technical expertise of man, far greater speeds could be reached than could ever be possible on the ocean above. Within minutes the train was hurtling through the darkness at twice the speed ever attained on the outward trip so that after a few more beers, a few more hours, a hearty meal of beef and potatoes from an extemporized kitchen—a blowtorch and an iron pot—they began to slow for the final stop.

Final it was, for the driver, knowing the urgency and in his enthusiasm, had stopped with his front wheels scant inches from the end of the track. In seconds Washington and Sapper had jumped down and clambered into the electric van for the short journey to the workface. Lights whisked by overhead in a blur while up ahead the sealed end of the tunnel rushed toward them.

"Better put these boots on," Sapper said, handing over a hip-high pair. "It is going to get wetter before it gets drier."

Washington pulled the boots on as they were stopping, and when he jumped down from the van, Sapper was already at the unusual device that stood to one side of the tunnel. While he adjusted the various levers and dials upon it, the van hummed into reverse and rushed away. Gus joined the small group of navvies there who greeted him warmly and whom he answered in turn, calling each of them by name. Sapper shouted to them for aid, and they rolled the machine closer to the tunnel wall and arranged the thick electric cables back out of the way.

"Ready whenever you say, Captain."

"Fire it."

When the head ganger pulled down the master switch a thin beam of burning ruby light lashed from the laser and struck high up on the rusted steel panel that sealed the tunnel's end. That this was no ordinary manner of light was manifest when the metal began to glow and melt and run.

"Stand to one side," Washington ordered. "The tunnel ahead is sealed off from the ocean, but it is still full of water under tremendous pressure. When the laser holes through we are going to have. . . ."

The reality of the experience drowned out the descriptive words as the intense beam of coherent light penetrated the thick steel of the shield, and on the instant a jet of water no thicker than a man's finger shot out, hissing like a hundred demons, as solid as a bar of steel, under such great pressure that it burst straight back down the tunnel a hundred feet before it turned to spray and fell. In the meantime Sapper had not been idle and his beam was now cutting out a circle of metal high up on the top of the shield, a circle that was never completed because the pressure on the other side was so great that the disk of solid steel was bent forward and out to release a column of water that roared deafeningly in their ears as it hurtled by. Now the tunnel was chilled and dampened by the spray of the frigid water and a vaporous haze obscured their vision. But the burning beam of light cut on, making an oblong opening in the center of the shield that extended downward as the water level lowered. When the halfway mark was reached, Washington got on the phone and radio link to the men at the Grand Banks Station end of the tunnel. Though they were no more than a tenth of a mile ahead there was no way to speak directly to them; his voice went by telephone back to Bridgehampton, from there by radio link across the ocean.

"Open her up," Washington ordered. "The water is low enough now and everything is holding."

"Too much for the pumps to handle," Sapper said as he looked down gloomily at the dark water rising around their ankles, for the water here had to be pumped back eighty miles to the nearest artificial island with a ventilation tower.

"We won't drown" was the only answer he received, and he twisted his elk's tooth in the earring as he thought about it. But at the same time he worked the laser until he had driven the opening down to the level of the rising water around them, where the beam spluttered and hissed. Only then did he enlarge the opening so a man could fit through.

"It won't get any lower for a while," said Gus, looking at the chill water that reached almost to his waist. "Let us go."

In a single file they clambered through, with Washington leading, and forced their way against the swirling water beyond. An instant later they were soaked to the skin and in two instants chilled to the bone, yet there was not one mutter of complaint. They shone their bright electric torches about as they walked and the only conversation was technical comment about the state of the tunnel. The joints were sealed and not leaking, the work was almost done, the first section of the tunnel almost completed. All that lay in their way was eight feet of frozen mud that formed the great plug that sealed the end of this tunnel and joined it to the sections beyond. All of the navvies carried shovels and now there was a use for them, for when the mud had been pumped in from the outside it had flowed part way back down the tube and was not congealed. They tackled this with a will, arms moving like pistons, working in absolute silence, and before this resolute attack the wet earth was eaten away, tossed to one side, penetrated. Their shovels could not dent the frosty frozen surface of the sealing plug, but even as they reached it, a continuous grinding could be heard—and then a burst of sound and a spatter of fragments as a shiny drill tip came thrusting out of the hard surface.

"Holed through!" Sapper called out and added an exuberant war cry that the others echoed. When the drill was withdrawn, Gus clambered up to the hole and shouted through it, could see the light at the far end, and when he pressed his ear to the opening he could hear the answering voices.

"Holed through," he echoed, and there was a light in his eyes that had not been there before. Now the navvies stood about, leaning on their shovels and chattering like washerwomen as the machine and men on the other side enlarged the opening from a few inches to a foot to two feet.

"Good enough," Sapper shouted through the tunnel in the frozen mud. "Let's have a line through here."

A moment later the rope end was pushed through and seized and tied into a sturdy loop. Washington dropped it over his shoulders and settled it well under his arms, then bent to put his head into the opening. The faces at the other end saw this and cheered again and even while cheering pulled steadily and firmly on the rope so he slid forward bumping and catching and sliding until he emerged at the other end, out of breath and red-faced—but there. More hands seized him and practically lifted him onto the waiting car that instantly jumped forward. He wrestled free of the rope as they stopped, then sprang for the elevator. It rose as he put foot to it, rattling up the shaft to emerge in the watery afternoon sunshine of the Grand Banks. Still more than a little out of breath he ran across to the level spot before the offices, brushing the dirt from him as he went, to the strange craft that was awaiting his arrival.

It is one thing to gather intelligence from the printed word and the reproduced photograph, to be deluded into the knowledge that one is acquainted with an object one has never seen in three-dimensional reality, yet it is another thing altogether to see the object itself in all the rotundity of its existence and realize at once that there is a universe of difference between the two. Gus had read enough to labor under the delusion that he knew what there was to know about a helithopter so that the reality that he was wrong caused him to start and almost stumble. He slowed his run to a fast walk then and approached the great machine with more than a little awe manifest in his expression.

In the first place the machine was far bigger than he imagined, as large as a two-decker London omnibus standing on end. Egg-shaped, oh definitely, as ovular as any natural product of the hen, perched on its big end with the smaller high in the air above, squatting on three long curved legs that sprang out of the body and that could be returned in flight to cunningly artificed niches carved from the sides. The upper third of the egg was transparent, and from the very apex of this crystal canopy there jutted up a steel shaft that supported two immense four-bladed propellers separated, one above the other, by a bulge in the shaft. Gus had barely a moment to absorb these details before a door sprang open in the dome and a rope ladder unrolled and rattled down at his feet; a head appeared in the opening and a cheery voice called out.

"If you'll join me, sir, we'll be leaving."

There was a lilt to the words that spoke of Merioneth or Caernarvon, and when Gus had clambered up to the entrance, he was not surprised to see the dark hair and slight form of an RAF officer who introduced himself as Lieutenant Jones.

"Your seat there, sir, those straps for strapping in, sir."

While he spoke, and even before Gus had dropped into the second chair in the tiny chamber, Jones' fingers were flitting over the controls, putting into operation this great flying engine. There was a hissing rumble from somewhere beneath their feet, a sound that grew rapidly to a cavernous roar and, as it did so, the long-bladed rotors above their heads stirred to life and began to rotate in opposite directions. Soon they were just great shimmering disks, and as they bit into the air; the helithopter stirred and shook itself like a waking beast— then leaped straight up into the air. A touch on a button retracted their landing legs while the tiny artificial island dropped away beneath them and vanished, until nothing except ocean could be seen in all directions.

"Being an engineer yourself, Captain Washington, you can appreciate a machine such as this one. A turbine, she has, that puts out two thousand horsepower to turn the contra-rotating rotors for a maximum forward speed of two hundred and seventeen miles in the hour. Navigation is by radio beam and right now we are locked onto the Gander signal and all I need do is keep that needle on that point and we'll be going there directly."

"Your fuel?"

"Butane gas, in the liquid form, very calorific."

"Indeed it is."

Within a matter of minutes the coast of Newfoundland Island was in sight and the city of St. John's moved smoothly by beneath them. Their route took them along the coast and over the countless bays that fringed the shore. Jones looked out at the landscape then back to his controls, and his hand reached out to touch a switch.

"Number one tank almost empty so I'll switch to number two."

He threw the switch, and the turbine rumbled and promptly died.

"Now that is not the normal thing I'm sure," said he with a slight frown. "But not to worry. I can switch to tank number three." Which he did and still the engine remained silent and they began to fall.

"Well, well, tank four." Which proved to be as ineffective in propelling the ship as had its earlier mates. "But we cannot crash, bach, there is that. We windmill down to a soft landing."

"Wet landing," Gus said, pointing out at the ocean.

"A well-made point. But there should be enough fuel left in tank one to enable us to reach the shore."

The flying officer seemed cheered by these final words because they were the first true prediction he had made in some time, for when he switched back to the first tank the turbine rumbled to life instantly and the helithopter surged with power. As he curved their course toward the shore he tapped, each in its turn, the dials set above the switch, then shook his head.

"They all read full; I cannot understand it."

"Might I suggest you radio the base at Gander about our situation."

"A fine idea, sir, would I could. No radio. Experimental ship, you know. But there, beyond that field, a farmhouse sure, perhaps a telephone, contact reestablished."

As though to defy his words the turbine coughed and stopped again and their forward flight changed to an easy descent. Jones hurriedly lowered the landing legs, and they had no sooner locked into position than the craft touched the ground in the center of a plowed field. Instants later the pilot had thrown open a door in the floor and had dived down into the maze of machinery below.

"That is very interesting," he said, spanner in hand and banging on the cylindrical tanks below him. "They are empty, all of them."

"Interesting indeed, and I shall report their condition if I can find a telephone at that farmhouse."

The hatch release was easy to locate and Gus pushed it open and threw the rope ladder out and was on it and down it even before the lower end had touched the ground. At a quick trot he crossed the field, angling toward the patch of woods behind which the farmhouse was located, running as quickly as he could across the stubble, running his thoughts no less quickly over the hours remaining before the train left London, the darkening sky above a dire portent of their vanishing number. Nine A.M. the train departed, nine in the morning and here he was on the other side of the Atlantic the evening before, running, which was not the most efficient form of ocean crossing imaginable. For the very first time he felt that he might not make it in time, that all the effort had been in vain—but still he kept on running. "Giving up" were two words he simply did not know.

A farm track, a wooden fence, and finally, reluctantly, the trees thinned out to permit a wood-framed farmhouse to come into view. The door was closed, no one in sight, the shutters drawn. Deserted? It could not be. With raised fist he hammered loudly on the door, again and again, and almost abandoned hope before there was the rattle of a moving bolt and it opened a crack to reveal a suspicious eye set in an even more suspicious face and, if a beard can be said to be suspicious, wrapped around about by a full and suspicious graying beard.

"Aye?" a suspicious voice muttered, nothing more.

"My name is Washington, sir, and I am in some distress. My flying vehicle has been forced down in your field and I would like very much to make a call with your telephone, for which you will be reimbursed."

"No telephone." The door closed far quicker than it had opened, and Washington instantly pounded upon it until it reluctantly opened for a second time.

"Perhaps you could tell me where the nearest neighbor with a phone—"

"No neighbors."

"Or the nearest town where a phone—"

"No towns."

"Then perhaps you could allow me into your house so we could discuss where I could find a telephone," Washington roared in a voice accustomed to giving orders over the loudest of background clamor. Where good manners had not prevailed this issuing of a command had, for the door opened wider, though still reluctantly, and he stamped after the owner into the house. They entered a modest kitchen, lit by glowing yellow lights, and Washington strode back and forth the length of it, his hands clasped tightly behind his back, while he attempted to discover from the reluctant rustic what his next step would be. A good five minutes of questioning managed to worm out the tightly held information that nothing could possibly be done in any reasonable length of time. The nearest town, far distant, the neighbors, nonexistent, transportation in fine, only equine.

"Nothing can be done then. I have lost."

With these sad words Gus smacked his fist into his palm with great force, then held his wristwatch toward the lamp so he could tell the time. Six in the evening. He should have been at the air base by now, boarding the Super Wellington for the jet flight to England, instead of in this primitive kitchen. Six, now, eleven at night in London and the train departed at nine in the morning. The light hissed and flickered slightly, and the hands on the watch irrevocably told the lateness of the hour. The light flickered again and Gus slowly raised his vision to the shade, the transparent globe, the glowing hot mantle within.

"What . . . kind . . . of . . . light . . . is . . . this . . . ?" he asked with grim hesitation.

"Gas" was the reluctant answer.

"What kind of gas?"

"In a tank. The truck comes to fill it."

The light of hope was rekindled in Gus' eye as he spun about to face the man again. "Propane? Could it be propane? Have you heard that word, sir?"

Squirming to hold in the fact, the farmer finally had to release it. "Something like that."

"It is that, because that is the only sort of liquid gas that can be used in the north because butane will not vaporize at lower temperatures. There is hope yet. I wish to purchase that tank of gas and rent your farm wagon and horse to transport it for me. What do you say to that, sir?"

"No."

"I will pay you one hundred dollars for it."

"Maybe."

"I will pay you two hundred dollars."

"Let me see it."

Gus had his wallet out on the instant and the bank notes smacking on the table. The head and the beard shook in a very definite and negative *no*.

"Colonial money. I don't take it. Canadian greenbacks or sterling, either."

"I have neither."

"I ain't selling."

Gus would not give in, not surrender to this backwoods agrarian; the man who had triumphed over the ocean would not admit defeat at the hands of a pastoral peasant.

"We will swap then."

"Whatcher got?"

"This." He had his watch off in an instant and dangling tantalizingly before the other's eyes. "A two-hundred-and-thirty-seven-dollar waterproof watch with four hands and seven buttons."

"Got a watch."

"Not a shockproof, self-winding, day-of-the-week-and-month-revealing watch that tells the time when this button is pressed"—a tiny bell struck six times—"and contains an infinitesimal radio permanently tuned to the government weather station that gives a report when this one is pressed."

". . . small craft warnings out, snow and winds of gale velocity. . . ."

A report he would just as well not have heard. Standing there, the watch of many qualities extended in silence until, with the utmost reluctance, a work-gnarled hand came up and, with the greatest trepidation, touched it.

"It's a deal."

Then physical work, a harsh anodyne to the frustration of impotent waiting, struggling with the ponderous tank by the light of a paraffin lantern, loading it into the farm cart, harnessing the reluctant beast, driving it down the track, pushing mightily to get it over the ruts in the field toward the lighted helithopter where Jones' head popped out of the open hatch when he was hailed.

"Found the trouble, sir, and strange it is since I filled the tanks myself. They are empty and the indicators somehow broken so they read only full. It could only be—"

"Sabotage. But I have the answer here. Propane, and may there be enough of it to reach the base at Gander."

It was the work of seconds to remove the access ports and reveal the hulking forms of the helithopter's fuel tanks. Jones spat on his palms and reached for his toolbox.

"We'll have to have these out since there is no way to transfer the fuel. If you will tackle the fittings above, Captain, I'll tackle the clamps and we'll have them pulled before you can say Rhosllanerchrugog."

They worked with a will, metal struck metal, and there was no further sound other than an occasional muffled curse when a wrench slipped and drew blood from barked knuckles. The tanks were freed and toppled out to the ground, after which with an even greater effort, they managed to raise the replacement tank into their vacated position.

"A lorry will return your tank and remove these," Jones said and received a reluctant nod in return.

Straps had to be arranged to secure the new tank in

position, and there was some difficulty in attaching the fitting to its valve, but within the hour the job was done and the last connection tightened, the plates lifted back into place. The wind had accelerated while they worked and now the first flakes of snow sped by in the lantern's light. Gus saw them but said nothing; the pilot was working as fast as he could; but he did glance at his wrist before he remembered his watch was no longer there. Surely there was still time. The new jet Wellingtons were rumored to do over 600 miles an hour. There *must* still be time. Then the job was done, the last fastener fastened, the last test completed. They climbed the ladder and rolled it up, and at the touch of the switch the great engine stirred and roared to life once more. Jones turned on the landing lights and in that fierce glare they saw the snow, thicker now, the frightened horse kicking up its heels against the wagon, then stampeding out of sight with the shouting farmer in hot pursuit while the rotors spun, faster and faster until they were up, up, and away into the blinding storm.

"Instruments all the way," said Jones with calm assurance. "There's nothing over five hundred feet high between us and the field so I'll hold her at a thousand, no need to waste fuel going higher. Follow the beam and keep an eye on the altimeter and that's all there is to it."

That was not all there was to it, for the weather worsened with every mile they flew until the great mass of the helithopter was tossed and spun about like a child's kite. Only the ready skill and lightning reflexes of the pilot held them on course while, despite his outward calm, the dampening of his shirt collar indicated the severity of the task. Gus said nothing, but held tight to the seat and looked out at the swirling snow as it blew through the golden cone of their lights, and tried not to think about the minutes quickly slipping by. There was still time; there had to be time.

"Now look at that, just look at that!" Jones called out cheerily as he spared an instant to point to their radio beacon where the needle was spinning in mad circles.

"Broken!"

"Not half likely—it just means that we are over the beacon, over the field. Hold tight for we are going down."

100

And down they did go, plummeting toward the unseen ground below while the altimeter unwound and the snow rushed by.

"Do you see anything, Captain Washington?"

"Snow, just snow and blackness. Wait . . . a moment . . . there! Off to port, lights of some kind, and more below us."

"Gander. And there come the lads to hold her down and just in time. Sit tight, for this is not ideal weather to maneuver."

But he did it. A fall, some quick work with the controls and throttle to check them, slow, drop again, until with a jar and a thud they were grounded and the engine died as the throttle was closed.

"I'll never forget what you have done, Jones," said Gus as he warmly shook the other's hand.

"Just part of the ordinary RAF service, Captain. A pleasure to have you with me. You'll win this yet."

But would he? After a quick rush through the blizzard to the haven of the heated building and hurried introductions by the officers there, Gus became aware of a general unease coupled with the specific disability of anyone to meet his eye.

"Is there something wrong?" he asked the Wing Commander in charge of the base.

"I am afraid there is, sir. I would be hesitant about taking off an aircraft in a storm like this, but it could be done, and the runways could be cleared of snow now, no trouble there. But I am afraid that the wind, gusting over a hundred miles an hour at times, has lifted and dropped the Wellington and damaged her landing gear. Repairs are being made, but I do not think they will be done before midnight at the earliest. We could still reach London in time, but if the storm continues unabated—and Met office says it will—all the runways will be sealed by then. It is the horns of the dilemma, sir, for which I beg your profound pardon."

Gus said something in return—he was not sure what—then accepted with thanks a steaming mug of tea. He looked into it and saw failure and drank deep of the bitterness of despair. The flyers sensed his mood and busied themselves at other tasks to leave him in solitude. It was so damnably frustrating!

So close, so much effort, so much rising over circumstance and fighting adversity, to be stopped at the last moment like this. The forces of nature had balked him where sabotage had not. These bitter thoughts possessed him so that he was scarcely aware of the room around him so that the officer who stood in front of him remained there for some minutes before his physical presence made itself known. Washington raised a face stamped with defeat until he became aware of the other man and smoothed his features so his feelings did not show.

"I am Clarke, sir, Captain Clarke. Forgive me for intruding with what may be, could be considered as, a suggestion."

He was a thin man, slightly balding, wearing gold-rimmed glasses, and seemed most sincere. His voice still held the softness and rolled r's of his Devonshire youth, though there was nothing of the rustic about him now.

"Please speak, Captain Clarke, for any suggestion is more than welcome."

"If I might show you, it would perhaps be simpler. If you would follow me."

They went through a series of connecting passageways to another building, for snow and blizzards were not unknown here at the best of times and this device enabled free passage whatever the weather. They were now in a laboratory of some sort with wires and electric apparatus on benches, all dominated by a mass of dark-cased machinery that covered one wall. Through glass windows set in the mahogany front of the impressive machine, brass gears could be seen, as well as rods that turned and spun. Clarke patted the smooth wood with undisguised affection.

"A Brabbage engine, one of the largest and most complex ever made."

"Beautiful indeed!" Gus answered in sincere appreciation, forgetting for the moment his great unhappiness. "I have never seen one this size before. I suppose you have a large memory store?"

"More than adequate for our needs as you can see." He opened a door with a flourish to disclose serried banks of slowly turning silver disks, all of them perforated with large numbers of small holes. Metal fingers riding on rods brushed the surfaces of the disks, bobbing and clicking when they encountered the openings. There was a continual soft metallic chatter going on, along with some hissing and an occasional clatter. From this welter of sound Clarke must have detected an inconsistency because he cocked his head to one side, listening, then threw open the next panel and seized an oil can from the bench behind them. "A fine device, although it does need upkeep." He dropped oil on the bearings of a cam follower where it rode up and down on the smoothly formed and complex shape of a brass analog cam. "They are making wholly electric Brabbage engines now, calling them computers as if that made a difference; they are much smaller but still filled with bugs. Give me good solid metal any time, although we do have trouble with backlash in the gear trains."

"It is all very interesting. . . ."

"Please excuse me, Washington, no excuse really, bit carried away, dreadfully sorry." He dropped the oil can, flustered, picked it up again, restored it to the bench, closed the panels and pointed to a door across the room. "If you please, now you've seen the Brabbage, right through here. This may interest you more."

It did indeed, for beyond the door was a great hangar, in the center of which stood the tall, spearlike form of a rocket. Fifty feet or more it reached up, six feet thick at the base, finned and sleek and stern, all of a color, blue-black and striking.

"Black Knight, our best and most powerful rocket. Completely reliable with a most efficient liquid fuel engine that burns kerosene mixed with peroxide. Very delicate controls. Sends back a radio signal as it goes along that is monitored by the Brabbage engine we have just seen, so that course adjustments can be made in flight. Using this we have been most successful in an experimental program that may soon become a standard practice. Rocket mail, the post office is interested, as you can well imagine, between here and Croydon. They have one of the electric computers there, pick up the signal as Black Knight comes over the Atlantic and guide her in, cut engines and all that, bring her down by parachute. . . ." His voice ground to a halt as Washington turned slowly to stare at him, fix him with a terrible gaze. When he spoke again, it was hurriedly, stumbling at times. "No, hear me out please, experimental program, nothing more. Worked every time so far, mail got through, but who knows. Tremendous acceleration. Kill a person dead perhaps. But other experiments, sent a chimp last time, Daisy, sweet thing, in the Regent's Park Zoo right now, never seemed to faze her, ate a whole hand of bananas when they took her out."

"If you are saying what I think you are saying, Clarke, why then I am your man. If you would like a volunteer to cross the ocean in your piece of fireworks, then I have volunteered. But only if it gets me there by nine in the morning."

And indeed that was what the Devonshire engineer had in mind and the more he explained the more convinced Gus was that victory might still be snatched from the already closing jaws of defeat. The other engineers and the base commander were called in and they conferred, London was contacted on the radio telephone and more conferring was done until, in the end, there were none to say nay and the yea-speakers were overwhelming in numbers, and there was no choice but to do this new and wonderful thing.

It was a labor to finish in the few hours that remained, but labor they did. Outside, the arctic storm howled and beat in impotent rage against the buildings while inside they worked on the device that would vanquish the storm, vanquish time and space and distance to send a man from the new world to the old in a matter of some few minutes. The rocket was fueled and readied and all of its complex circuitry tested while, high above, the mechanics labored to install the rubberized lining and to pump in all the gallons of water that would be needed.

"That is the secret," Clarke explained, eyes glistening with enthusiasm behind the smudged lenses of his glasses. "Amniotic fluid, a secret known to nature and there for the taking had we but the sense to know where to look. But we have at last looked and seen and utilized this secret. As you know, one G is the force of gravity, gravity as we know it on the surface of the Earth. Acceleration and gravity seem to be identical, or at least that's what that German chap Einstein

104

who used to be at Oxford says, identical. We accelerate and feel two G's and are uncomfortable, three G's and we suffer, five G's, six G's strange things happen, death and heart failure and blackouts, very nasty. But, suspended in a liquid medium, we have had test subjects, simians for the most part, subjected to fifty G's and they survived in fine fettle. So that is what we are doing now. A space-going womb, ha-ha, you might call it."

"Submerged all the way? I hope I won't have to hold my breath?"

"That would be impossible . . . Oh, pulling my leg, Captain Washington? Oh, dear, yes! No, indeed, quite comfortable. The water may be chill, but you will be wearing a wet suit with an oxygen mask. Quite comfortable indeed."

Comfortable was not exactly the correct word, Gus thought as helping hands slipped him into the space-going bath. He dropped below the surface and fastened the snaps to his belt as he had been instructed while he breathed slowly and carefully through the mask. It was all quite interesting, though there was a moment of disquiet when the distorted faces and hands above him vanished and the nose cone slid into place with a resounding clang. The water carried all the sounds, and he could hear the clanking and grinding of metal as the bolts were secured. Then silence.

This was the worst part, the waiting in the darkness and solitude. Alone, alone as he had never been before in his life, perched atop this column with its cargo of highly combustible fuel. Waiting. He could visualize the roof opening up above the rollers, the preflight checkoff, the switches thrown. He had been told this would take a few minutes but had not realized that his time perception would be thrown off to such a degree. Had minutes passed—or hours? Had there been a failure, an accident? Could he escape from here or would he die in a boiling pot atop a fiery column? His imagination steamed along in high gear and had he been able to speak he would have shouted aloud so great was the tension at this moment.

And then a sound, a whine, and a scream like the souls in the pit in eternal agony. He felt the hair on his neck stir before he realized that it was just the high-speed pumps going into operation, forcing the fuel into the combustion chamber. The flight was beginning! And at the instant he realized that, there was a distant rumble and roar that grew fantastically until it beat at his ears so he had to cover them with his hands while something unseen jumped on his chest and battered him down. Blast off!

For a long and unmeasurable time the pressure continued—then suddenly ceased as the engines shut down. The rocket was coasting. In those eternity-long minutes while the engines were working they had burned their way up through the storm and penetrated the atmosphere above and the stratosphere above that until now they were beyond the last traces of airy envelope of the Earth and arcing through the vacuum of space. The Atlantic was a hundred, two hundred miles below them and ahead was England. And the waiting computer at the airport in Croydon, that sleepy little suburb of London, an electric Brabbage engine that was not as reliable as the mechanical one and he hoped that, at least this once, the enthusiastic Captain Clarke would prove to be wrong about the reliability of that machine.

Yet as they coasted, his heartbeat slowed, and he felt a measure of peace and even good cheer. Fail or succeed, this was a voyage that would be remembered, almost a modern version of that romantic novel by the Frenchman about a voyage around the world in eighty days using all forms of transportation. Well, here he was, utilizing some forms of transportation that the redoubtable M. Verne had never dreamed existed. This game was certainly worth the candle. It was in this reposed state of mind that he felt the engine reignite and so composed was he that he smiled at the thought. Dropping now, over Surrey and down, steering, pointing, falling, and at the last moment the crack of the released parachute. There was a sudden jar that might well have been that parachute opening and soon after another and what he was sure was a cessation of motion. Had he arrived?

Evidence came swiftly. There was a clank and a bump, then another one and once again the grinding of metal. In a moment the nose cone above him vanished from sight and blurred faces appeared in its place against the brilliant blue of the sky. Of course! He had flown into daylight in the swiftness of his voyage. He rose up and pushed his face above the surface of the water and tore off the mask and smelled the sweetness of the warm air. A smiling face, bad teeth in that wide grin, and a spanner in the matching hand, looked down, while next to this face a sterner one below a blue official cap and a square of cardboard next to that.

"Her Majesty's customs, sir. You have seen this card which lists contraband and dutiable items. Do you have anything to declare?"

"Nothing. I have no baggage."

Strong hands helped him out to the top of the wheeled platform that rested against the tall rocket. A view of white concrete, green trees beyond, a waiting group of men, distant cheers. He turned to the customs officer.

"Might I ask you the time?"

"Just gone a quarter to nine, sir."

Was there time? How far to the station in London? Ten, twelve miles at least. Pushing away the helping hands, he scrambled to the ladder and half slid to the ground, stumbling at the bottom and turning to see a familiar bulky form before him.

"Fighting Jack!"

"Himself. Now hurry and you like t'make it yet. There are clothes in here." He thrust a paper parcel into Gus' hands while hurrying him forward at the same time toward an unusual vehicle that was backing toward them.

"That there driver is Lightning Luigi Lambretta who is a good driver, even though a Wog. Now get in and away with you."

"A pleasure to meet you, *signore*," the driver said as Gus dropped into the empty cockpit and felt the seat slam into his back the instant he was done. "This car the winner of the Mille Miglia, so not to worry. *Due cento,* two hundred of your horsepowers, like the wind we shall go. Steam-powered turbine, fueled with gasoline and using freon as the vaporizing fluid. The *polizia* out and roads cleared all the way to Putney Bridge and beyond. A nice day for the drive."

They roared, they raced, they dived down the road with a squeal of complaining rubber as they sideslipped and skidded broadside into the London Road at over a hundred miles an hour. Quick glimpses of bobbies holding back the crowds, flags waved, a holiday air to everything. Squirming in the tiny seat, Gus managed to slip out of the wet suit, and the slipstream grabbed it and whisked it from sight. He was more careful as he opened the parcel and drew out smallclothes, shirt and tie, and a lounge suit, sturdy boots below all this. It was an exhausting effort to get them on, but don them he did and even knotted his tie fairly adequately.

"The time?" he shouted.

"One minute past the nine."

"Then I have failed. . . ."

"Not yet, *signore*." Roaring at 135 miles an hour onto the Putney Bridge. "Things are arranged, I have talked by the phone, all of England is on your side, the queen herself. She was delayed leaving Buckingham Palace, marvelous woman, and now she proceeds most sedately by the horse and carriage to the station. All is not lost yet."

Would he succeed? Would failure follow this heroic effort? It was now in the hands of the gods, and it was to be hoped that they were smiling. Brake, accelerate, squeal of rubber, broadside through the narrow streets, a twist of the wheel to save the life of a stray dog, around another corner and there was the station. Down the ramp toward the platform, the State Coach to one side, empty.

The train, pulling out.

"Never fear, *dottore*. Lightning Luigi will not fail you!"

Laughing like a drain and twisting his fierce mustachioes with one hand, the intrepid driver hurtled his blood-red machine at the platform while the officials and bystanders scattered, raced up to the train, alongside of it, easing over until his offside wheel was only inches from the platform edge, matching his speed to that of the train and holding it steady and even close to the open door.

"If you would please to disembark, *signore,* the end of the platform fast approaches."

In the instant Gus was standing on the seat, standing on the rounded top of the racing car and bracing himself with a hand on the driver's head, reaching out for the extended hand from the train, grabbing it, leaping, looking back horrified as the driver stood on his brakes and slid and twisted and slammed into the pillars at the station's end. But he was waving and shouting happily from the smoking wreck.

"This way, sir," said the porter. "Your seat has been reserved."

II. POINT 200

Green England hurtled by outside, fields and streams like speeding patchwork quilts, blue rivers that swept under their wheels, black bridges and gray stone villages nestled around church spires, also in motion, also whisking by to quickly vanish along with the waving crowds in the fields and the rearing horses and barking dogs. It seemed that the entire countryside was unrolling for the benefit of the lucky travelers in this mighty train this fortunate day, for so smooth was the ride that the passengers aboard the *Flying Cornishman* felt that they were indeed standing still and the whole of England was spinning by beneath them for their edification alone.

They were indeed a blessed few who had secured passage on this inaugural run of the tunnel train, nonstop London to Point 200, the artificial island far out in the Atlantic Ocean, west of Ireland, and over a hundred miles from the nearest shore. The queen was aboard, and Prince Philip, while the Prince of Wales also had returned by special train from Moscow where he was on a state visit to make the trip. There was a sprinkling of the nobility and the Proper Names, but not as many as might be expected at the Derby or a fashionable opening, for this was science's day, the triumph of technology, so that the members of the Royal Academy outnumbered those of the House of Lords. The company directors were there as well as the largest financial backers, and a well-known actress whose liaison with one of these backers explained her presence. There was champagne, bottles of it, cases of it, oh dear—a refrigerated room full of it, courtesy of The Transatlantic Tunnel Company who had bought almost the entire stock of an excellent 1965 from a lesser known but superior chateau. This golden liquid flowed like a river of beneficence through the corridors and compartments where glasses were lifted and toasts drunk to the glory of this hour, the superiority of British engineering, the strength of the pound, the stability of the Empire, the peace of the world, the greatness of this day.

Aboard as well, in sorely diminished ranks, was the press, thinned down by the exigencies of seating space, swollen again by the need for complete world coverage for this historical event. One cameraman was filming everything for the entire world to see at the same time on their television sets, though of course BBC viewers would see it first, while the world papers would have to be satisfied with what the gentleman from Reuters told them, other than the French, that is, who would read what was written by a small dark gentleman, pushed to the rear by his bulkier Anglo-Saxon colleagues, who was aboard though by bribery for which at least one head would roll in Transatlantic House. Of course the gentleman from the *Times* was there, since the kind attentions of the Thunderer of Printing House Square were much sought after, and a few other leading journals including, with much reluctance and persistent insistence since this was going to be a *transatlantic* tunnel, the square-shouldered bulk of the New York *Times'* man.

They all wanted to talk to Washington at once, because he was the most singular piece of news aboard for the readers around the world who had been following every thrilling and heart-stopping detail of his journey. Now, on the last leg, with the finish line but a few hours away, they wanted him to describe all of the earlier stages down to the smallest detail. Between sips of champagne he answered them, reliving the heart-stopping moments aboard the helithopter and the rocket, the mad ride to London, the last-moment arrival. He was informed in turn that the driver, Lambretta, had received only minor bruises and regretted nothing, was in fact enthused by the fact that one of the more popular dailies had already purchased his personal story for a price reputed to be in five figures. Every foot of the journey to Penzance, Gus was interviewed, and he was rescued only by the fact that the journalists had to file their stories. Since they would have tied up completely the only telephone and telegraph link from the train they had been forbidden access to them, with the exception of the gentleman from the *Times* who had been permitted to file one brief report, so arrangements had been made to put off a bag in Penzance. The great canvas sack, boldly labeled "Press," was quickly filled with the reports and stories and the can of film put in on top. Other arrangements of an ingenious nature had been made as well so that the various reporters now dispersed to complete the work. Fast cars were waiting by certain fields, displaying flags of particular colors, ready to pick up dropped containers, one motorcyclist on a racing machine paralleled the train briefly on a stretch of road and was seen to end up in a pond still clutching a hoop and attached package he had seized, while more than one net-armed and speedy boat waited in waters the train would cross.

Free of his interviewers for the moment, Gus found his compartment and his allotted seat, which he now saw for the first time, and accepted the congratulations and another glass of champagne from the other passengers there. At this point he escaped their attention, for the train was slowing as they passed through Penzance where the waiting thousands cheered uproariously and waved their Union Jacks with such animation that they fluttered like gaudy birds. The press bag was thrown to the platform and the attendant telegraph men, the train picked up speed again, through the city and toward the dark mouth of the tunnel, passing the sidings where the other trains waited, packed with humanity, to follow after the inaugural run. Faster and faster it went to dive with a roar into the black opening, accompanied by excited female shrieks at the sudden night. Gus, who had been in a tunnel before, closed his eyes when they entered and when the others had exhausted the pleasures of gazing out at nothing and turned back he was well and soundly asleep. They appreciated his fatigue after the voyage he had just accomplished and lowered their voices accordingly so that he slept the sleep of the just, and they only roused him when the announcement was made that they were just ten minutes from arrival at Point 200.

An air of electric excitement overwhelmed the travelers and

even the most cynical and worldly wise were possessed by it, peering out at the darkness, getting up and sitting down again, and generally displaying an eagerness they would normally have scorned. Slower and slower the great train went until a grayness could be seen ahead and then, startling and sudden, a burst of brilliant sunlight as they emerged from the tunnel into the open air. Through the empty trainyard and over the points they rumbled to the station where the waiting band struck up the lively tune of "Tunnel Through the Deeps," the song specially commissioned for this occasion from Sir Bruce Montgomery and now having its debut performance. Wide and clean and spacious this station was, and seemingly empty of life until the passengers poured from the train, oohing and ahing at the appointments. For the top of the station, high above, was constructed entirely of large panes of glass through which blue sky and soaring gulls could be seen. This was supported by cast-iron columns enameled white and decorated at the junctions and on the capitals by iron fish and squid and whales cunningly cast into the fabric of the supports themselves. These configurations were finished in blue, and this color scheme of white and blue was carried on throughout the great station, giving it an airy and light feeling out of all proportion to its size.

The passengers held back respectfully as the red carpet was brought up and unrolled and the queen and her party descended. There was the quick flashing of lights from the photographers and then they had gone and the others followed.

No one, no matter how stern of demeanor or inflexible of expression, but failed to hesitate for a moment and to draw in a gasp of breath upon emerging from the station between the alabaster columns that supported the portico. For here was a vista that was breath-catching and inspiring, a wholly new thing come into the world. Broad white steps descended to a promenade that glistened and shone with the multihued splendor of the inlaid mosaics, arches, and waves and wriggling bands of color not unlike those of the promenade at Copacabana Bay which undoubtedly had no small influence upon their design. Beyond this was a field, a rolling meadow of the trimmest and greenest grass that sloped down gently to

113

the deep blue of the ocean beyond that was now breaking with small waves upon the shore. No flotsam or refuse marred the purity of this ocean so far from any shore, no land was visible at any distance in any direction where only the white wings of the yachts scudding across the surface broke the perfect emptiness. Once the visitor descended these steps there were greater wonders to come, for this promenade followed the shore of this new island and with every step forward there was something incredible to see.

First a great hotel stretching long wings into a flower-filled garden below and rising in matched, blue-domed towers high into the air. On the terrace here the orchestra played a dance tune to tempt passersby to the linened tables where black-garbed waiters stood ready to pour the tea. There was a holiday air about this spot and along the promenade, a holiday holding its breath in the wings and waiting to arrive, for all of this was ready and had never been used before, brought in by sea and constructed here in all optimism that custom would follow when the tunnel was opened. Restaurants and dance halls, and tucked away behind the elegant establishments, little lanes that led to fun fairs and round-abouts and ferris wheels, coconut shies and public houses; something for everyone. Farther along were the beaches of white sand that glistened welcome, and soon the first bathers could be seen, stepping hesitantly into the water then shouting in amazement for here, in the middle of the Gulf Stream, the water was warm and salubrious as it never was at Brighton or Blackpool. Behind the beaches rose the turrets and towers of Butlin's 200 Holiday Camp waiting impatiently for all who had booked in, the loudspeakers already calling the first arrivals to the heady pleasures of group amusements. And more and more, until the eyes of the strollers were filled with the color and panoply. Farther on, around the island, there was the yacht basin, already jolly with the jostling boats that had sailed here for this grand opening day, and still farther along a tree-crowned hill where the promenade ended in an outdoor bowl where a Greek drama, ideal for this pastoral setting, was about to begin. All was pleasure to the eye and so it had been designed, for the hill shielded from view the other half of the island where the industrial park, railway sidings, and commercial docks were located. Great things were planned for Point 200 and the transatlantic tunnel, and the investors had flocked to its proffered charms. It was indeed a wonderful day.

Washington enjoyed the stroll and the sight of the colorful activity just as well as did the shopkeeper from Hove or the lord from his castle, walking and mingling with them along the way. Tired finally, he repaired to the great hotel, The Transatlantic Towers, where a room had been reserved for him. His bag, sent on ahead weeks ago, had been opened and unpacked, while the table was banked with flowers and congratulatory telegrams. He read a few then put them aside, feeling let down after the fury of the preceding hours, sipped from the champagne provided by the management and went to his bath. Soon after, feeling refreshed and in better sorts, he donned a lightweight silk tropical suit, more fitting for this clime than his tweeds, and was just fixing his cravat when the telephone chimed. He took it from the drawer, put the microphone on the table before him and the receiver to his ear, and threw the small switch which activated it. The familiar voice of Drigg, Lord Cornwallis' secretary, spoke, congratulating him on his voyage and extending the marquis' invitation that he join them on the terrace at his convenience.

"I will be there shortly," Gus said, disconnecting the instrument, putting a flower in his buttonhole, and drinking one last glass of champagne in preparation for the encounter.

It was a small and elite group that was gathered there on the secluded balcony overlooking the sea, taking the late afternoon sun and basking in the balmiest of breezes. A sideboard spread with regimented bottles enabled them to help themselves to whatever drink they chose without a waiter to interrupt their privacy. If a pang of hunger should stir them, a great crystal bowl of Beluga caviar rested in cracked ice for their edification. Above the sideboard there hung in stately display a detailed map of the North Atlantic with the route of their tunneling ventures scribed upon it, upon which, from time to time one or the other of the men would rest his eyes and usually smile at that heartening sight. Sir Isambard Brassey-Brunel sat with coat open and his waistcoat half unbuttoned, an unusual relaxing of sartorial standards for him, and sniffed from time to time at the sweetness of the sea breeze and took small sips from his glass of Perrier water. Across from him Lord Cornwallis relaxed with a slightly more fortifying drink of Hennessy Seven Star of an unbelievable vintage, varying his attention between this and a Jamaican cigar of impressive length and girth and superior whiteness of ash. Sir Winthrop Rockefeller considered the hour too early for such spirituous beverages, so sipped instead from a glass of claret with the bottle placed handily beside it. All three men were composed and given almost entirely to small talk, basking in the relief of a job well done before turning their energies to the next task ahead. For all of the news was good, they had nothing to fault, it was indeed a splendid day.

When Augustine Washington was shown in, they rose by common consent, and the handclasps that were exchanged were those of mutual acclaim. They did congratulate the young engineer on the success of his voyage that so dramatized the opening of this new age of tunnel travel, and he in turn thanked the financiers for making everything possible, and the older engineer for the design and labor that had enabled the tunnel to be done at all. Sir Isambard nodded at this tribute, aware of what was his rightful due and, after they had seated themselves and Gus had accepted a glass of wine from Sir Winthrop's bottle, composed himself to speak about a matter he had long considered.

"Washington, we have been estranged long enough. Our personal differences have not prevented us from doing our best for the company, but I do feel that the past is now so much water over the dam and it is time to let bygones be bygones. Rockefeller here is chairman of the American board again, and I want to state before these gentlemen that you have done an excellent job with the American tunnel." He sipped from his glass for a few moments while the two other gentlemen cried *hear, hear!* with great enthusiasm, then resumed. "When I am wrong I freely admit it, and now I admit that the technique of preforming and sinking tunnel sections is not as dangerous as normally assumed and is indeed faster as you have proven. It has been utilized in completion of the tunnel we passed through today as proof

116

of this assumption. It is my hope that we shall be able to work together more closely in the future, and, in addition, you will find yourself welcome in my house once more."

This latter bit of information took Gus by surprise, for he started from his chair, then sank back again, and a slight pallor touched his skin, proof that this casual piece of social intelligence caused more stir in his constitution than the most severe of the hazards through which he had so recently passed. However, he took some of the wine, and when he spoke next, he appeared as composed as ever.

"I accept this news and this invitation with the most profound thanks, sir, because, as you must know, I still consider you the leading engineer and builder of our age and it is my pleasure to work under you. It will also be my pleasure to call at your home. And your daughter is at home, I presume. . . ."

"Iris is well, and she accompanied me on this trip, and I presume will make you welcome as well, but I do not discuss this sort of thing with her. Now to other and new business. Though today is a success, tomorrow will surely come with its problems and we must prepare for it. The two units of the tunnel now completed are important and will, if the figures I have seen are correct prognostications, earn money in their own right. Point 200 will soon grow to a major and most modern port where goods bound for England can be off-loaded and sent ahead by train, quickly and surely, thus avoiding the channel traffic and the outmoded facilities of the Port of London. I believe we have witnessed its other success today as a spa and resort. On the far side of the Atlantic the Grand Banks Station will perform like functions, in addition to which the fishing fleets will unload their catches there for rapid transport of fresh fish to the colonies. All well and good, but we must press on and justify the name of this company. We must cross the Atlantic. The preliminary surveys and reports are done; now is the time to finalize and put them into action."

There were warm shouts of agreement at this, for they were all as eager as he to see this mighty project through to completion. Financing would, of course, be the next consideration, and the two chairmen of the transatlantic boards of directors rose and spoke in turn about the state of their treasuries. In fine they were healthy as bull pups. The recent improvement in the states of their national economies, that might very well be traced to the tunnel operations, had left considerable profits in a number of hands and eager money was waiting to be invested. That the nods of agreement were not quadrilateral was not noticed in the warmth of their enthusiasm; there seemed nothing standing in their way. But Gus grimly fingered the stem of his glass, looking up betimes at the map on the wall, then down at the surface of his wine as though some important revelation was drowned in its depths. He seemed at internal battle within himself, as indeed he was, for a door had opened again this day that had been closed for many a year and for this he would be eternally grateful. But what he had to say might very well close that door again—yet he could not leave this place without speaking, for it was scientific fact that he must mention. And so the war of heart and head was fought within and, silent as this battle was, it was more terrible and devastating than any conflict of shell or bomb. In the end he came to a conclusion for he drew himself up, drained the prognosticatory glass of wine, and waited for an opportunity to speak. This came soon enough as the financial details were resolved and the engineering programs came to the fore. He gained the floor and crossed to the map where he traced the proposed course of the tunnel with a steady finger.

"Gentlemen, you all realize that the longest and most arduous portion of our labor now lies before us. Sir Isambard has proposed a radical form of transportation in these sections of our tunnel and research has proven that his genius was correct. The evacuated linear electric line will add a new dimension to transportation in the future."

"Forgive my interruption," said Cornwallis, "but I'm not quite sure that *I* understand the operation of this thing and I would be deeply grateful if you could explain it in some manner that would enable me to grasp it. Though I can wend my way through the intricacies of international finance I must admit that my head grows thick at the mention of electrons and allied objects."

"Nonsense, Charles, I've told you a dozen times how the

118

blasted thing works," Sir Isambard broke in, quite warmly. "Let's get on with the affairs at hand."

"Please, an explanation first, if you don't mind," said Sir Winthrop with some gratitude. "I am happy to see I am not alone in my ignorance, which was causing me some concern. If you would, Washington."

Sir Isambard subsided, grumbling at this outrageous waste of time, draining a reckless draft of his spring water, so annoyed was he. Gus took this as assent and explained.

"The theories behind the proposals are quite complex, but there is no need to go into that since the results can be simply understood. Think of the tunnel, if you will, as an immense length of pipe, solid and integral. There is air in this pipe at the same pressure as most air upon the surface of this world, that is in the neighborhood of some fifteen pounds to the square inch. This air serves only one function, that of permitting the passengers in the trains to breathe, an important fact to the passengers but of no importance to the engineering of the tunnel. These few pounds of pressure add nothing to the structural strength of the tunnel walls to keep out the immense pressures of the ocean above, and from the engineering point of view the air is in fact a handicap because it limits and retards the speed of the trains. Remove the air, an easy thing to do, and the trains would go faster while using less power."

"But the people, sir, our passengers, they must breathe!"

"And breathe they will—for the trains will be sealed and pressurized just like high-altitude aircraft. With the air removed we can now consider higher speeds than were ever possible before. Why, there is no reason why our trains cannot go eight, nine hundred—even a thousand miles an hour."

"Wheels and bearings will not sustain such speeds."

"Perfectly correct, Sir Winthrop, which leads us to the next stage. A train with no wheels. This train will literally float in the air as powerful magnets in the train are repelled by equally powerful magnets in the track. We have all seen how one magnet will support another in midair upon its repelling field, and thusly will our train ride in its evacuated tunnel. But what will move our train? And here is the genius of Sir Isambard's answer. The train will move by means of a linear traction engine. I shall not explain this complex invention, but suffice to say it is like an electric motor turned inside out with one part of the motor aboard the train and the other stretched on the roadbed the length of the tunnel with no physical connection needed or wanted between them. In addition, most of the train's speed will be derived by its dropping off the edge of the continental shelf and falling the three miles down to the abyssal plain on the ocean's bottom. And there you have it, gentlemen, a sealed train in an evacuated tube, floating in midtunnel and touching nothing physical, even molecules of air, being started on its way by gravity and continuing by electricity. A form of transportation as modern as the entire concept of the tunnel itself."

There were sighs of relief from the financiers and a few questions to clear up certain points so that when Gus continued he had the informed and knowledgeable attention of his small audience.

"As has been demonstrated we now have our means of transportation and the preforming technique to lay the tunnel. The final step, before detailed surveying and construction begins, is the selection of the route to be followed. Because of the complex nature of the ocean's floor, great care must be taken at this point, for the bottom of the Atlantic is no sandy lagoon that may be slashed directly across. Hardly! What we have here is a varied landscape more complex and drastic than the one we know on the dryer surfaces of our globe. There are, of course, the abyssal plains that form the bottom, lying at an average depth of sixteen thousand feet below the ocean's surface, but other features must be taken into consideration. Down the center of the ocean runs the Mid-Atlantic Ridge, a great mountain chain that is in reality a double row of mountains with the gorge of the Rift Valley between them. These mountain ranges and the Rift Valley are crossed at right angles by immense canyons called fracture zones that resemble wrinkles in the Earth's hide. Other features also concern us, the Mid-Ocean Canyon, like an underwater riverbed on the ocean's floor, seamounts, and islands and trenches—that is, extraordinarily deep gulfs—such as this one, on the map here, that is over five miles in depth. And there are more factors to consider,

120

underwater earthquakes and vulcanism which are concentrated in specific areas for the most part, the very high temperatures of the sea bottom near the Rift Valley as well as the fact that the sea bottom here is moving as the continents drift apart at the rate of about two inches a year. It appears, and the geologists confirm the suspicion, that new matter rises from the Earth's interior in the Rift Valley and spreads outwards at that steady rate. All problems, gentlemen, but none of them problems that cannot be surmounted. You will note the proposed route on this map which avoids these enumerated obstacles. If we begin here at Point Two Hundred on the edge of the Continental Shelf, our tunnel proceeds roughly north northwest along the fracture zone we call forty-one G that joins the end of the Mid-Atlantic Ridge and the offset Reykjanes Ridge south of Iceland. By doing this we avoid the peril of crossing the Rift Valley which ceases to exist at this point. Now, farther west, we emerge from the fracture zone and turn south, skirting the Mid-Ocean Canyon and swinging around the heights of the Milne Seamount until we reach the Sohm Abyssal Plain. At this point the tunnel will turn almost due north to rise up the Laurentian Cone to meet the tunnel already laid on the Continental Shelf at the Grand Banks Station. Now this route might be said to have a few faults."

There was a rumble like a distant storm from Sir Isambard's direction that Gus chose to ignore as he continued.

"Since the ocean bed is so warm in the fracture zone special tunnel sections will be laid on the bed itself, not in a trench, and constructed in such a manner that water will circulate through cavities in them to keep them cool. However, the major criticism might be that, in order to avoid all the geological details, the tunnel will be twice as long as it would be if it went in a direct manner, therefore twice as costly."

"Good God, man," Sir Isambard exploded. "We have been over this before and you know we can't go directly across the infernal ocean. So what are you suggesting?"

There was a hushed silence as Gus took a sheet of paper from his pocket and unfolded it; gulls could be heard crying outside and the strains of the orchestra playing in the distance, but all was listening quiet on the balcony.

"That is just what I am suggesting," said Gus, with a positive sureness. "And I intend to show you how. I propose that the tunnel go due *south* from Point Two Hundred, over the flat bed of the Biscay Abyssal Plain to a base in the archipelago of the Azores, where it will meet the other leg of the tunnel that has come almost due east from the Grand Banks along the Oceanographic Fracture Zone. This route is less than half the length of the one under consideration now and, in addition, will provide an unexpected benefit. Cargo can be unloaded in the Azores base to be loaded on ships for Africa and the continent, thereby shortening the voyage greatly. Plus the fact that another leg of the tunnel can eventually be considered from the Azores to Spain that will make a train connection between the Continent and the Americas. If this is done, the results will be simply amazing. It will then be possible for a passenger to board a train at the Pacific port of Provideniya at the end of the Trans-Siberian Railroad and thence to proceed by train across Siberia, Russia, and Europe, under the Atlantic, across America and connect with the Trans-Canada Railroad to Alaska, there to finish his journey once more on the shores of the Pacific. After a journey around at least ninety-nine percent of the Earth's circumference at this point."

At this juncture there were shouted questions and eager enthusiasm for more information about this novel idea until Sir Isambard hammered with his fist for silence.

"A mad dream, nothing more. Or rather it would be possible were it not for the aforementioned Mid-Atlantic Ridge with the Rift Valley which, I believe, is at least one mile wide and a number of miles deep at this point. It cannot be crossed. The plan is discarded."

"Not so. The valley can be crossed and I have the plan for that procedure in my hand. It will be crossed, gentlemen, by an underwater bridge."

Into the following silence Sir Isambard's snort of contempt burst like a trumpet peal. "Nonsense, sir! Poppycock and nonsense! A bridge cannot be built a *mile long* that will support the weight of the tunnel sections at this depth."

"You are correct, sir, it cannot. That is why this bridge will have *negative* buoyancy, a thing our tunnel sections have in any case until we weight them down, so it will float over the canyon, secured in place by heavy cables."

This time the silence was absolute as Gus snapped open his plan and put it before them, explaining how the bridge would be made and how, since it floated, it could absorb the two-inch-a-year movement of its opposite ends, and all the other details of his new proposal. For every question asked he had an answer and it soon became obvious that, unless unknown factors were thought up, this plan was far superior to the earlier one in every way. Long before this became clear to the others it was realized by Sir Isambard who parted the table and stood, arms folded, staring out at the setting sun. When the others had exhausted their words and enthusiasm and stopped for breath, he turned and fixed Gus with a gaze the coldness of which outdid the most frigid blast of arctic night.

"You have done this deliberately, Washington, produced your plan to supersede mine in an attempt to obtain some gain."

"Never sir! You have my word. . . ."

"There is no doubt this design or a variation of it will be adopted," the redoubtable man continued, unheeding of the interruption. "The tunnel will be built to the Azores and you will get the credit, I am sure. Since I put the good of the tunnel above my own ambition, I will continue working as I have in the past. But for you, sir, personally, sir, I have little regard. Please be informed that you will no longer be a welcome guest in my house."

Gus was nodding even before the other had finished, for it had been foreordained.

"I was sure of that from the beginning," said he, a weight of unspoken feelings in these simple words. "I have nothing but good feelings for you, sir, nor do I intend to do you injury in any way. I wish that you would believe me when I say that I have put the good of the tunnel ahead of any personal advancement for myself. Therefore, in the light of your remarks, I have no choice other than to resign from my position in The Transatlantic Tunnel Company and leave their employ. If my presence is a disconcerting one and interferes with the completion of this great work, then I will remove that presence."

His remarks, though spoken in a quiet voice, brought a stunned silence to the others in the room, though only for a few moments to Sir Isambard.

"Resignation accepted. You may leave."

This further paralyzed the verbal apparatus of the two men of finance so that Gus had actually risen from his chair and was on his way to the door before Lord Cornwallis could speak.

"Washington, a moment, if you please. We must not be unilateral, matter of precedence, full consideration, blast me, I am not sure what to make of all this." With an effort he assembled his fractured thoughts and sought for some form of compromise even at this last moment. "We have heard your suggestion and must consider it, since, Sir Isambard, with all due respect, you cannot speak for all the members of both boards or even for myself or Winthrop. What I would suggest, what I do suggest, sir, is that we here consider what must be done and will then inform you of any decisions reached. If you would tell us where you could be reached at the end of our conference, Captain Washington?"

"I will be in my room."

"Very good. We will contact you as soon as there are any results to our deliberations."

Gus left then and the heavy door closed behind him with a powerful clack of the latch and a certain positive finality.

III. A BRIEF ENCOUNTER

On all sides cheer and goodwill abounded; tastefully clad couples and groups talked animatedly, friends called to one another with hearty voices, bellboys darted through the press in the lobby with messages and telegrams undoubtedly all of a happy, wholesome nature, and such a flood of good spirits encompassed them all that it must surely have lapped up and out of the windows and across the pavement, bringing smiles as it went and causing even the gulls on the balustrades to cry with joy. Yet through this ocean of cheer one dark vessel plunged, a man with an aura of great unhappiness about him, cut off and alone, architect of all these glories, and now, in the hour of triumph, set apart from all those who enjoyed the fruits of his labors.

Washington was too depressed to be depressed, too numb for feelings, even miserable ones. He walked steadily and calmly with a grave exterior which in no way indicated the depths of unplumbed unhappiness within him, for the tunnel had become his life and without it he felt an empty shell. He was tempted to be bitter toward himself, yet if he had it to do over again he knew he would do the same. The improved route must be used. If saving the tunnel meant a loss in his personal life, then it must be done. Occupied like this, in the darkest of dark studies, he plowed through the crowd to a berth before the lift doors and waited for them to open. And open they did, quickly enough, for this lift was powered by hydraulics with a piston sunk into a cylinder deep in the ground, and he stepped aside so the single occupant could emerge, face to face with him, a chance of fate, a roll of some celestial die that determined that the occupant should be none other than the lady so recently mentioned, Sir Isambard's daughter Iris.

"Iris," said he, and could say no more for to his eyes her face and elegantly garbed form were enclosed in a golden nimbus that made detailed vision difficult.

"You're looking older, Gus," said she with the eminently more practical vision of a woman. "Though I must say that touch of gray to your hair does add something." But, practical as she was, it could not be denied that, sure as her voice had been when she started to speak, there was a certain indeterminate waver to it before she had done. At this all conversation ceased and they stood, simply looking at each other for long moments until the boy who operated the lift piped up.

"Lift going up, your honor, all floors, if you please."

With this they stepped aside so others could enter and in that bustle of humanity they were as alone as they might be in a rushing sea. She was as radiant as she ever had been, Gus realized, more beautiful, if that were possible, with the new grace of maturity. His eyes moved of their own accord down her left arm to her hand and fingers, but there any revelatory vision was blocked by the kidskin gloves she wore. But she was well aware of his gaze and its import and she smiled in answer.

"No ring, Gus. I still live with my father, very quietly."

"I have just left him and we have talked. We had most friendly words and then, I am afraid, most harsh ones."

"My father in all truth."

"The friendly ones encompassed an invitation to make myself a guest at his home again. The harsh ones. . . ."

"You shall tell me of them later, for just the first will do for now." With simple foresight she knew that this moment, brief as it might be, must be clutched at and abstracted from the flow of time. What came after would arrive speedily enough, but the passport to social intercourse granted by her father had to be seized and utilized. "Is there no place we can sit for a few moments?"

"I know the very spot," answered Gus, knowing nothing of

126

the sort, but also now aware that here was an opportunity that might be grasped and therefore clutching at it with both hands. He excused himself for the moment and addressed one of the functionaries of the establishment who was stationed nearby, and if a sum of money changed hands this was to hurry the arrangements, which it apparently did, for they were led without further ado to a secluded alcove at the rear of one of the dining rooms where an attendant waiter vanished as soon as he had taken their order and filled it with unusual speed. No tea this time, as on their last meeting, for Iris had reached her majority in the meanwhile and was one of the new brand of liberated women who drink in public places. She had a Tio Pepe sherry while he perforce had a double brandy.

"To your good health, Iris."

"And to yours, which needs it more since you seem to treat health and life with a very cavalier attitude."

"This last trip? It was necessary and there was little risk."

"Risk enough to one who sits in the quiet of a London room and waits for the reports and wonders if the next one will be the last."

"You are still concerned about me?"

"I still love you."

The words were spoken with such sincerity and truth that they bridged the gap of years as though these years had never existed, they had never been parted. His hand found hers, eagerly waiting, and pressed it beneath the table.

"And I have never stopped loving you, not one moment of the time. May the waiting be ended now. I still carry your ring, here, and have always hoped that I could return it to you some day."

"And can you now?"

The loosening of his touch, the moving away of his hand from hers told her more surely than any words could what was to be.

"I can, only if you will break with your father."

"The harsh words you spoke of. Yes, I suppose you must repeat them now, though I wish to heaven I did not have to hear them." With this she drained her glass and her cheeks glowed with the drink and the power of her feelings. Gus admired her in silence before he spoke again, knowing there was none like her on the face of the globe, knowing he would never love another.

"I have proposed certain changes in the tunnel that will modify and even alter drastically parts of your father's plan. We are of different opinions regarding the changes. He feels, and perhaps it is true, that my modifications of his work are a personal attack, and after offering me the courtesy of his home, he has withdrawn the offer. That's where matters now stand." No power on Earth could have dragged from him the admission at this point that he had also resigned from the tunnel, since this would be crude playing upon her sympathies.

"They stand there indeed and stand very crookedly, I must say. Ring for another drink, if you please, because it is not every girl who sees her dreams restored and dashed again all in the space of a few brief minutes."

When she had her sherry and had touched it to her lips, he spoke the question that meant the most to him.

"Must they be dashed? You are past twenty-one now and your own person. Would you marry me despite your father's displeasure?"

"Dear Gus, I would if but I could. But I must stay by him."

"But *why*? Can you give me any reason?"

"Yes, one, and I tell you only because you should know that I do this not from any lack of love for you, but because I have a certain duty. My mother is dead, as you know, my two brothers engineers like yourself and always far away. I am the only one he has. What I say now is in strictest confidence, known only to myself and his physician, some trusted servants. My father is not a well man. Oh, I know he bombasts and roars and carries on as he always did, but the years have exacted their toll. He has had a heart attack, a serious one, so serious he lay between life and death for days. Now I must look after him and smooth everything in his way that I can because the physician says the next one will be fatal; he is almost certain of that. If I left him, went against

128

his will, I would be killing him as surely as if I pulled a trigger."

After that there was nothing that could be added. They sat in silence for a few moments, then she rose and he stood as well. She kissed him on the cheek softly, and he returned this distant embrace which is all they would allow themselves, knowing the wellsprings of emotions that they would tap with anything more. They said good-bye, and she left and he watched her go until she vanished from sight behind the gilt pillars, then he resumed his seat and the swift destruction of his glass of brandy which burned so warmly, the only warmth in a world of cold, that he ordered another to follow it, then the bottle for the table so the waiter would not have to run back and forth so often.

Yet as much as he drank, he was immune to drink. The level in the bottle lowered until it faced extinction and still its potent medicine never touched the chill core within him. His work had vanished, the one he loved had gone, there remained only an encompassing despair. He sat in this manner for a great length of time until he became aware of the waiter standing at his shoulder, holding out a portable telephone instrument while a mechanic connected it to a concealed fitting in the wall.

"You are wanted on the line, Captain Washington," said he.

Cornwallis came on, his voice loud and booming.

"Washington, is that you? What a relief, we have been trying to contact you now for hours."

"Yes?"

"Well, tried to contact you, as I said. Had quite a time here, I can assure you; Sir Isambard is a difficult man, as you well know. But he came around in the end. He puts the tunnel ahead of all other considerations as do we all. As I hope you do, too, Washington."

"Sir!"

"Of course you agree. In which case we are asking you to withdraw your resignation and carry on with us. We need you, man! Sir Isambard will build the Point Two Hundred to the Azores leg, the easier one, and will let you do the

American section with your infernal tunnel-bridge across the Rift Valley. Will you do it? Will you stay with us?"

The silence lengthened and Cornwallis' anxious breathing could be heard on the line. Despite the brandy he had drunk Gus was sober on the instant, and when he answered there was only firmness in his voice.

End of the Second Book

Book the Third

A Storm at Sea

I. ANGRA DO HEROISMO

Far out to sea thunder rumbled like great wooden kegs rolling over cobbles, and jagged flares of lightning lit up the banks of dark clouds with an ominous glow, creating for a moment an unreal landscape of fiery black meadows in the sky, a country of the damned hanging over the slate-gray sea. The first fat drops of rain flew ahead of the storm and splatted on the stone of the dockside while the gusts of wind sent up a shaking rustle and a clatter from the tall palm trees that stood in ranks along the shore. The tugs entering the harbor hooted hurried signals one to the other with white puffs of steam from their whistles, the steam silently visible to the watchers on shore long seconds before the mournful moan of the whistle could be heard. They had reason to hurry, for already the approaching storm was raising the waves and breaking streamers of white spray from their tops. Yet they still must make haste slowly, for the great whale of a tunnel section they had in tow resisted any hurried motions with its multi-hundred-tonned mass. Its humped back was just awash so that the rising seas broke over it, giving it the appearance of some surfacing sea monster, gray and ominous. Finally, with careful attention and much frantic hooting, it was brought into safe harbor behind the sea walls and secured to the waiting buoys there.

From his vantage point on the raised platform of the Control Office, Gus had a clear view of the harbor and workyards, trainyards and barns, junctions and tracks, cranes and constructions, slipways and storehouses; a varied industrial landscape that was all under his control, where thousands of men labored at his bidding. It was a familiar scene now, yet he never tired of it. The radio at his elbow reported the successful tying up of the tunnel section at the same moment his eye saw the rising column of steam, the long blast that meant the tow was completed and the lines could be cast off. With this finished he lowered the powerful binoculars and wiped at his fatigued eyes, then looked around at the boom and bustle that was his life. Riveting guns hammered and metal clanged on metal, cables squealed as great traction engines moved ponderous weights, small whistles toot-tooted as the puffing yard donkeys scurried back and forth through the maze of tracks, shunting the goods wagons about, great cranes swung as they lifted cargo from ships' holds. The raindrops came closer and closer until they were upon him, and now he was grateful for their cool touch upon his bronzed skin, for it had been a hot and close day. Though his shirt, with the sleeves rolled up, and his puttees were made of the thinnest cotton khaki twill, the heat had still been insufferable, so that the rain was a welcome change. He even took off his topee and turned his face up to the sky so the drops splashed pleasantly upon him. Only when the shower became a torrent did he seek shelter in the office and take up a towel to dry himself. The office staff continued with their assigned tasks, except for the head ganger, Sapper Cornplanter, who now approached, carrying an immense sheaf of papers.

"I have all the work reports and time sheets for all the gangs, time and hours, days sick, everything. Heap big waste of time."

"I am forced to admit that I share your lack of enthusiasm—but what must be done must be done." He looked at his watch and came to a quick decision. "Have a messenger take them to my hotel and leave them at the desk so I can work on them tonight. New York is concerned about the rising unit costs and the secret of the higher expenses may well be here. I'll go over them this evening and see if I can prise out the nugget of truth from this dross of statistics. In fact, I shall leave now before the shift ends so I won't be trampled underfoot.

"Making tunnels is thirsty work in this climate. Navvies need plenty of beer, wine, red-eye, to keep going."

"A point I'll not argue. You know where I'll be and what to do."

The quick storm had almost passed as he picked his way across the yards, the last drops clattering on his topee. He needed his knee-high engineer's boots here, for the mud was constantly churned up by the heavy lorries. Reaching Avenida Atlantica, the wide street that ran along the shore, he strolled down it, blending with the heterogeneous crowd that was now making its appearance after the warm afternoon siesta. He enjoyed this time of day, this parade of people from every walk of life, from almost every corner of the world, for it was his tunnel that had turned the sleepy little subtropical city of Angra do Heroísmo, on the island of Terceira in the Azores, into the bustling, brawling, international port it had become.

Of course the off-shift navvies were there, from both sides of the Atlantic, handsome in their scarves and colorful waistcoats, high boots and great hats, pushing their way through the pack and giving ground to no man. The olive-skinned islanders seemed in a minority here, but they did not complain because prosperity was now their lot, a prosperity never known before when fish were the only profit they took from the sea, not tunnelers' wages. Once the cash crops of pineapples and bananas, oranges, tobacco, and tea were sold on a perilous world market. Now these products were consumed locally with great enthusiasm, so that little or none had to be shipped abroad. Nor were the navvies the only customers of local goods, for where the tunnel went and the money from the men's pay packets, there went as well men and—alas!—women who had designs upon that money, whose only ambition in life was to transfer as much of it as possible from the purses of the honest working men to depths of their own sordid wallets. Gamblers there were in the crowd, sleek men with dark clothes, neat mustaches and white hands—and ready derringers on their persons to confront any man so rash as to dispute the honesty of a deal or the fall of a pair of dice. Moneylenders there were, who had ready cash at any time for any man gainfully employed, who exacted such immense sums in interest, three and four hundred percent

135

not being uncommon, that the Biblical injunctions against usury could be easily understood. Merchants came, too, not men of established business who displayed their wares in public and stated their price clearly, but gray men with folding boxes and velvet bags in secret pockets, who produced rings and watches, diamonds and rubies, at ridiculously low prices, inferring or whispering that the goods were *lava*—hot, that is; stolen, that is—though it would take an insane thief to steal such poor wares, for the rings turned green, the watches stopped ticking when the roaches inside them died, the diamonds and rubies fell to smithereens of glass if dropped. And there were women, oh, yes, hapless creatures of the night, betrayed, stolen, enslaved, entrapped, doomed to a life of hell that does not bear describing on the printed page lest the ink that forms the words grow warm, then scorching hot enough to burn the letters from the paper, for the eye of the gentle reader dare not behold the facts of such as these and the trade they plied.

All these were upon the sidewalks this afternoon, and more as well; Moorish traders come with dhows from Africa and Iberia bringing food, for the few islands of the archipelago could not produce enough for the great numbers of men based here, dark-skinned, hawk-nosed men in white burnouses who paced the pavement with firm tread, hands resting on cruel knives, interested in this strange outpost of the alien Christian. An occasional frock-coated man of business could be seen, for much business was conducted here, proceeding incognito in his uniform clothes so the observer could not tell if he was French or Prussian, Russian or Pole, Dane or Dutch. And more, and more they passed in an ever-changing, never-changing, flood of humanity.

Gus always enjoyed the show, and when he came to his favorite establishment, El Tampico, he turned in and sat at a table on the porch, just a few feet above the street, resting his arm on the thick brass rail that surrounded it, waving to the bowing owner and smiling at the rushing waiter who was bringing a chilled bottle of the local wine he favored, *vinho de cheiro,* a delicately scented, sweetly flavored wine that had the taste and smell of roses. He sipped at this and felt at peace. The work went well; there was nothing to complain about. But as he watched the crowd, he was aware, out of the corner of his eye, of someone sitting at the next table, back to him, moving very close. That this arrangement was not accidental was made manifest when the man, for it was a man, spoke in a low voice that only Gus could hear.

"Your navvies good workers, Meestair Washington, work very hard and need to eat very much. Feed them you must, beeg meals, beeg money. I joost happen to have many tons of canned hams, such good hams you would not believe and I have a sample here in pocket to prove you." Something slapped the table wetly, and Gus could not help noticing the piece of meat on a cloth napkin that had suddenly appeared at his elbow. He ignored it as well as he had ignored its owner, yet the man persisted. "See how fine, my, good pig from the mountains of the Balkans, eat, eat, you will enjoy. I have these hams to sell for special price for you, oh, good price, and under the table for you a certain commission, gold most suitable, yike!"

The speaker had terminated his conversation in this unusual manner because Sapper Cornplanter had appeared silently behind him and had lifted him suddenly by trouser seat and nape of neck and had hurled him bodily into the street where he instantly vanished. With his fingertips Gus sent the portion of meat after its master where it disappeared into the maw of one of the long-legged island dogs who roamed the pavement.

"More tons of concrete cut with sand?" Sapper asked, still standing but pouring himself a glass of wine for his services.

"Not this time. From the little I heard before you terminated the conversation it was either a stolen shipment of meat, or tainted or some such. They never stop trying, do they?"

Sapper grunted a monosyllabic answer and faded from sight inside the café. Gus sipped at his wine. The entrepreneurs would never believe that he could not be bribed; it was their lifetime of experience that everyone had his price, everyone was accessible, so they persisted in trying with him. He had long since stopped trying to talk to them, so arranged that one of his men was always near by when he was in public and that a certain gesture of his hand, apparently meaningless in itself, carried the information that once again a conversation never begun was due to be terminated. He forgot about this matter at once, so common had it become, and had more wine while the gentle tropical evening drew on apace. When he was refreshed and cooled, he made his leisurely way through the still-streaming crowd to the Terra Nostra Hotel where he kept a room, the best hotel on the island, which was by no means an extravagant claim, as well as being hideously overcrowded as were all hotels and restaurants since the tunnel had located here. The manager, bowing with pleasure, for Gus' custom was greatly respected, handed over the package the messenger had brought, and Gus went up to his room to do some work on the papers before partaking of the late dinner so favored by the islanders.

When he unlocked the door, he saw that the room was dark, that the chambermaid had neglected once again to turn on the light. This was a normal occurrence and he thought little of it as he closed the door and groped for the switch and threw it. Nothing happened. The electricity must be off again, he thought; the coal-fired generating plant was hideously inefficient. Yet the lights had been on in the lobby. Puzzling over this, he had just turned back to the door when the sudden glare of an electric torch burned into his eyes, the first intimation he had had that he was not alone in the room. Whoever his secret visitor might be, he was certainly here for no good end, that was Gus' instant thought, and he turned to hurl himself at the light source. He was stayed from attacking by the silent appearance of a man's hand in the beam, a hand clutching a nickel-plated and very efficient-looking revolver.

"You are here to rob me?" said Gus, coolly.

"Not exactly," the secret visitor answered in what were obviously American tones. "Let us say I wished first to see who you were, then to make sure you were alone, and lastly the gun, if you will excuse its presence, to ensure you did nothing hasty in this darkened room as, I believe, you were starting to do."

"Here is my wallet, take it and leave. I have nothing else of value to you in the room."

"Thank you, no," said the voice in the darkness, a hint of laughter to the words. "You misconstrue my presence." There was a rattle and a clatter at the lighting fixture, though the torch stayed steadily on Gus all the time, and the lights finally came on.

The nocturnal visitor was a man in his middle thirties, garbed in the almost traditional dress of the American tourist abroad: colorful, beaded Indian shirt, peaked fisherman's cap with a green plastic visor that was studded all over with badges and patches indicating places he had been, knee-length shorts, and sturdy, hobnailed boots. Around his neck was slung his camera and ancillary photographic apparatus, and from his belt there hung the required wire recorder that lectured him day and night on what he was seeing. His face was cheerful enough when he smiled, as he was doing now, but it hinted that in repose the icy blue eyes were stern, the wide jaw set, the broken, hooked, sharp nose might resemble the predatory bill of a hawk. Gus examined the man slowly and carefully, standing motionless under the ready threat of the revolver, looking for an opportunity to turn the tables. That this would not be necessary was proven an instant later when the stranger touched the bottom of his wire recorder so that the case fell open and a secret compartment was disclosed. Into this opening he pushed the gun while, at the same time, he removed a smaller object. The leather case sealed again with a click as, still smiling, he passed over the extracted metal shield.

"A pleasure to make your acquaintance, Captain Washington. My name is Richard Tracy and I am manager of the New York office of Pinkerton's. That is my shield you have in your hand and I was instructed, as further identification, to give you this note."

The sturdy envelope was closed with sealing wax, with Sir Winthrop's seal upon it, and showed no signs of having been tampered with. Inside was a brief note in Rockefeller's own hand which Gus recognized at once. The message was succinct.

This will introduce R. Tracy, Esq., whom I have retained privately. He is to be trusted absolutely in the matter to hand. W. Rockefeller.

"Do you know the contents of this letter?"

"Just the gist of it, that I am conducting an investigation and only you are to know about it. I was advised to inform you that Sir Winthrop has engaged me personally, out of his own private funds, and that you are the only other person who knows of my existence."

"I suppose you wouldn't care to tell me just what it is you are investigating?"

"Just getting to that, sir. Sabotage it is, a very nasty business indeed. I can cite instances you know of, and still more that you don't."

"Such as the mysterious lack of fuel in the helithopter in Canada?"

"True enough. And the cut cable on the tunnel section of the last part to the Grand Banks Station, the collapsing shed in the railyard, and many others. I have been here on the island for a little time now and have made an investigation in depth. There is a strong organization that is actively operating against the success of this tunnel. They are well financed and ruthless and will stop at nothing."

"But, who is doing this—and why?"

"At this stage I could only guess, and guessing is a thing I prefer not to do, being a man of facts and facts alone. Perhaps that is one of the things we will soon discover, for I have approached you now for your aid. I and my operatives have been investigating here for some months. . . ."

"I had no idea!"

"Nor should you have, for my men are of the best. You have seen some of them working on the tunnel, I'll wager, because I have managed to get them into a number of places. And now one of them—he is called Billygoat because he is as ugly and nasty as one—has been approached by the saboteurs and has agreed to aid them. That is where I need your help. You must supply me with a place to commit willful and expensive sabotage so that Billygoat will be admitted to their ranks. Once I know who they are we can swoop and grab the lot."

"It will take some thinking, but I know we can come up with something. I'll talk to—"

"No one, sir, no one if you will, for I value my life dearly."

"I miss your meaning."

"I will be frank. Other investigators have been hired in the past, and they either failed in their tasks or were found dead under mysterious circumstances. Sir Winthrop believes, and I agree heartily, that someone within the company is in league with the saboteurs."

"It cannot be!"

"But it is. Someone with much special knowledge, perhaps more than one person. Until we find out we take no chances, that is the reason why I came to your room in this strange manner. Other than yourself and Sir Winthrop, no one knows I am on the job."

"Surely I can tell—"

"No one! It must be that way."

It was agreed; no one else was to know. A system of passwords and means of contact were agreed upon, and an exuberant kind of sabotage worked out. When all was done, the secret investigator flipped open what appeared to be an identification bracelet on his wrist, but which proved to be a two-way radio with which he spoke to a confederate who disclosed that the room was not being watched. Armed with this knowledge, he turned off the lights and slipped out the door to vanish as mysteriously as he had appeared.

Though Gus worked late upon his papers and should have had all of his attention there, his thoughts kept returning to the mysterious saboteurs. Who were they—and who inside the company was part of the dastardly plan?

He found it hard to sleep when finally he retired, for his thoughts went around and around this bone of knowledge and worried at it unceasingly.

II. THE PLOT REVEALED

Not a sound disturbed the sunlit afternoon, not a word was spoken that could be heard, not a hammer struck metal, no sound of footstep or motor or any other man-made noise contrived to break the near-perfect stillness. Yes, waves could be heard slapping against the seawall while gulls cried overhead, but these were natural sounds and independent of man, for it was the men and their machines that were quiet all through the immense spread of the tunnel works as everyone had ceased his labor and climbed to some point of vantage to watch the drama being played out before their eyes. Every wall and roof and crane had men hanging from it like clusters of grapes, human fruit wide-eyed and silent in the presence of tragedy, staring fixedly at the small humpbacked submarine that was churning its way out of the harbor at top speed. Only at the highest vantage point of the Control Office was there any movement and sound, one man, the radio operator, throwing switches and touching his dials, clutching his microphone tightly, speaking into it, while great drops of perspiration rolled down his forehead and dropped unheeded onto the bench.

"Repeat, this is a command from Captain Washington. Repeat, you must abandon ship at once. Do you read me, *Nautilus*, do you read me?"

The speaker above his head crackled and sputtered with static, then boomed out with an amplified voice. "Sure and I can't read you, you not being a book and all, but I can hear you that well as if you were sittin' at me shoulder. Continuing on course."

A sound, something between a gasp and a sigh was drawn from the listening men while Gus pushed past them and

142

seized the microphone from the operator and flipped the switch to *speak*.

"Washington here—and this is an order, O'Toole. Lock your controls at once and bail out of that thing. I'll have the launch pick you up. Over." The airwaves hissed and crackled.

"Orders are meant to be obeyed, Captain Washington, but begging your pardon, sir, I'm thinking I'll just not hear this one. I've got old *Naut* here cranked up for more knots than she ever did before in her rusty life and she's going along like Billy-be-damned. The red's still rising on the meter, but she'll be well out to sea before it hits the danger mark."

"Can't you damp the pile?"

"Now I'm afraid I'll have to answer that in the negative, sir. When I turned on the power the damping rods just pulled all the way out and I haven't been able to get them back in, manually or otherwise. Not being an a-tomic engineer I have no idea how to fix the thing so I thought it best to take her out to sea a bit."

"Lock the controls and leave—"

"Little late, Captain, since everything is sizzling and sort of heating up in the stern. And the controls can be set for a level course and not for a dive, and dive is what I'm doing. Take her as deep as possible. So I'll be signing off now since the radio doesn't work underwater. . . ." The voice thinned and died, and the microphone fell from Gus' hand with a clatter. Far out to sea there was a flurry of white as the sub went under. Then the ocean was empty.

"Call him on the sonarphone," said Gus.

"I've tried, sir—no answer. I don't think he has it turned on."

Silence then, absolute silence, for the word had been passed as to what was transpiring and everyone there now knew what was happening, what one man was doing for them all. They watched, looking out to sea, squinting into the sun where the submarine had gone down, waiting for the final act of this drama of life and death being enacted before their eyes, not knowing what to expect, but knowing, feeling, that although this atomic energy was beyond their comprehension, its manifestations would be understandable.

It happened. Far out to sea there was a sudden broiling and

seething, and the ocean itself rose up in a hump as though some ancient and evil denizen of the deeps was struggling to the surface, or perhaps a new island coming into being. Then, as this evil boil upon the ocean's surface continued to grow, a fearful shock was felt that hurled men from their feet and set the cranes swinging and brought a terrible clangor from the stacked sheets of steel. While all the time, higher and higher the waters climbed until the churning mass stood hundreds of feet in the air and then, before it could fall back, from the very center there rose a white column, a fiercely coiling presence that pushed up incredibly until it was as high as the great peak on the nearby island of Pico. Here it blossomed out obscenely, opening like a hellish flower until a white cloud shot through with red lightning sat on top of the spire that had produced it. There it stood, repellent in its concept, strangely beautiful in its strangeness, a looming mushroom in the sky, a poisonous mushroom that fed on death and was death.

On shore the watchers could not take their eyes from the awful thing, were scarcely aware of the men beside them, yet, one by one, they removed their hats and held them to their chests in memory of a brave man who had just died.

"There will be no more work today," said Gus, his voice sudden in the silence. "Make the announcement and then you all may leave."

Out to sea the wind was already thinning and dispersing the cloud and driving it away from them. Gus spared it only one look, then jammed on his topee and left. Of their own accord his feet found the familiar route to the street and thence to El Tampico. The waiter rushed for his wine, brought it with ready questions as to the strange thing they had all seen, but Gus waved away bottle and answer both and ordered whisky. When it came, he drained a large glass at once, then poured a second and gazed into its depths. After a number of minutes he raised his hand to his head in a certain gesture and the guardian form of the great Indian appeared in the doorway behind and approached.

"Nobody here to give the bum's rush to," said Sapper.

"I know. Here, sit and have a drink."

"Red-eye, good stuff." He drained a tumbler and sighed with satisfaction. "That's what I call real fire-water."

"Have come more. In fact you can have the bottle. Stay here and drink for a while—and don't follow me. I'm going inside and out the back way."

The Indian puzzled over that for a moment, then his face lit up in a wide grin. "Say, now that's what I call a good idea. Just what an Indian does. Get woman to drown sorrows. I'll tell you best house. . . ."

"That's perfectly fine, but I'm old enough to take care of myself. Now just sit here."

Gus fought back a smile as he rose; if only Sapper knew where he was going. Without looking back, he went through the dining room and up the stairs that led to the rest rooms. However, after he had entered the dark hallway he stopped and listened to see if he was alone. When he was sure that he had not been followed, he went swiftly and quietly to the window at the end of the corridor and pulled it open; it was unlocked and well greased and opened silently. In one swift motion he was through it and balanced on the ledge outside, closing it behind him before he dropped into the dark alleyway beyond. He had not been seen; blank, cracked walls faced him and noisome refuse barrels stood close by. There were people passing at the sunlit end of the alley, none looking in, yet to be completely sure, he waited until the street there was empty. Only then did he run silently across to the other building, to the door recessed there that opened as he approached and closed behind him.

"It went all right? You weren't seen?" Tracy asked.

"Fine, just fine. Sapper is guarding my flank."

The Pinkerton man nodded and led the way to another room, well lit by electric bulbs since the shutters were closed and the curtains drawn. There was a radio set upon a table here and a man sitting before it who turned and rose as Gus entered.

"Sure and I feel like a departed spirit," O'Toole said.

"You did an excellent job."

"It's the actor in me, sir, and you were no slouch yourself. Why for a while there I was convinced that I was really back

on the old *Naut* and sailing her out for a deep six and it fair
to choked me up. She was a good ship and 'tis a pity she had
to go like that."

"A noble end, and far better than the breaker's yard where
she was headed. Her glands were beginning to leak and
fissures develop in her pressure hull. This way her destruction
served a good purpose."

"Yes, I'm sure you're right, though I have to mind the
danger from all that radiation that the technical manuals
warn us about."

"There is no worry there. The meteorologists assure us that
the prevailing winds will carry the radiation out to sea away
from the shipping lanes, and that the radioactive materials in
the sea water will be dispersed and harmless."

"An encouraging thought. So with that taken care of the
next order of business will be the grand adventure you are
embarking on this evening—that will give some meaning to
the demise of the dear old *Naut*. Can I go with you?"

"No!" said Tracy in a commanding voice, his fingers
lingering near the butt of a revolver that had been pushed
into the front of his belt and concealed by his jacket.
Another man, who had been sitting quietly in a chair in the
corner rose swiftly, and it could now be seen that a gun had
been in his hand all of the time. Tracy waved him back. "At
ease, Pickering, he won't be coming with us. Captain Washington, when I gave permission for another man to be
informed of events, it was with the firm understanding that
he would remain in this room until circumstances had run
their course."

"And so he will, Tracy; I gave you my word." He turned
back to the submarine pilot who was looking on with a fair
degree of incomprehension. "It has to be that way, O'Toole.
You have come into this matter blind, just taking my word
that sabotaging your own sub and sending her out to sea to
blow up and pretending, by radio, that you were aboard her,
was important—and highly secret. Perhaps you have some
hint of what is involved, but I ask you to keep it to yourself
if you do. And remain in this room with Pickering, for your

own good, if for no other reason. We are up against desperate men, and we must needs be as desperate ourselves and it is my firm belief that either of these two men would shoot you dead rather than permit you to leave this room this evening."

Both of the secret operatives nodded silent agreement while O'Toole shrugged in submission. "So be it, sir. Since I've committed suicide once today I'll not be wanting to do it twice."

"Sit under this light," Tracy told Gus, the matter ended and the revolver buttoned from sight again. "No one must recognize you or the game is up."

Under his skillful fingers Washington changed into someone else, so abruptly and efficiently that O'Toole breathed the names of a saint or two as he watched the transfiguration. First brown dye, rubbed well into his hands and face, then pads were slipped inside his cheeks, some brisk work with a dark pencil to accent lines in his skin, invisible rings put into his nostrils to widen and round them, all of this climaxed by a thick black mustache attached with spirit gum with a wig to match. When Gus looked into the mirror he gasped, for a stranger looked back at him, a Latin gentleman, one of the islanders perhaps, bearing no resemblance to the man who had sat first in the chair. While he admired this handiwork, Tracy was busy on his own face, working the same sort of transformation, climaxing the entire operation by producing two pin-striped suits with wide lapels and stuffed shoulders, definitely of a continental cut, as well as black, pointed shoes. After they had changed into the clothes, O'Toole let a thin whistle escape through his teeth.

"Why sure and I could pass you in the street and never know, and that's the truth."

"We must leave now," Tracy said, looking at his watch, calmly accepting the praise as his professional due. "We must use a roundabout route to reach the meeting place."

Darkness had fallen while they prepared their disguises so that the side streets and alleys that Tracy preferred were blacker than pitch. But he seemed to have acquainted himself with the underworld geography of the city for he made his

147

way unerringly to their goal. As they paused, outside a darkened doorway no different from a hundred others they had passed, he bent close and whispered.

"These are bloodthirsty men and sure to be armed. I have a second revolver, if you wish."

"No, thank you. I am a man of peace, not war, and abominate the things."

"A necessary tool, no more. But I have heard that your right cross was much respected in college boxing and more than once you were urged to enter the professional ring. If it comes to close work, there is nothing wrong with fists."

"I agree and look forward to the opportunity with pleasure. Now—lead on."

The door proved to be the back entrance to one of the fouler drinking dens that lined the waterfront, though it did have a balcony overlooking the main room where the gentry, or those who passed for it, could drink in a measure of solitude while watching the steaming stew of life below. They took a table at the rail, and Tracy waved back two dark-eyed and rouged women who began to sidle toward them. The waiter brought a bottle of the best the house offered, a thin and acid champagne at a startlingly high price, and they touched it to their lips without drinking. Speaking around his glass, in a voice that only Gus could hear, Tracy said, "He is there, the table by the door, the man who is drinking alone. Do not turn to look at him for there are other watchers here besides us."

Casually lighting a thin and dangerous-looking black cheroot that Tracy handed him, Gus threw the match onto the soiled floor and looked offhandedly down at the crowd. Drinking, shouting, gambling, swearing, it was a noisy bustle of life, a mixture of local toughs, navvies, coarse seamen, a den of a place. Gus let his eyes move over the man at the table just as they had moved over the others, an ugly man with a perpetual scowl, the agent Tracy had referred to as Billygoat. He was garbed as were the other navvies, for he had been working on the tunnel, at the waterfront section. He could have had access to the submarine which had first originated the idea in Gus' mind. His sabotage theoretically successfully finished, he was waiting for his payoff, waiting to meet others in the sabotage gang since now, by his drastic act, he had proved his worth.

It was then that, out of the welter of voices below, Gus made out one that sounded familiar, a bull-like roar that he was sure he had heard before many a time. He allowed his eyes to roam across the crowd again and controlled himself so he gave no physical sign of what he saw, but instead finished his slow survey and raised his glass. Only when the glass was before his face did he speak.

"There's a navvy down there, Fighting Jack, my head ganger from the English end of the tunnel. If he recognizes me. . . ."

"Pray he does not, for we are lost then and the entire operation must be scrapped. I know he arrived today with a levy of men for the English tunnel, but why of all the odds did he have to pick this establishment out of the many of its type to do his drinking? It is just bad luck."

And there was worse luck to come, as a hoarse bellowing in the street outside indicated. The door crashed open and through it came Sapper Cornplanter, more than three sheets in the wind, the full bottle Washington had ordered earlier that evening now almost empty in his hand. If anyone there had managed to miss his noisy arrival, he informed them now with a warbling war cry that set the glasses dancing on the bar.

"I can lick any man in the house! I can lick any three men if no one man has guts to stand up! I can lick any six men if no—"

"That is a heap big Indian bag of wind."

As these words were uttered Sapper froze and his eyes narrowed as he slowly turned his head in the direction of the speaker, moving with the deadliness of a swiveling gun turret, his eyes as menacing as twin cannon. As he did this Fighting Jack climbed to his feet. In the balcony above Gus stifled a groan as Sapper answered.

"And you are a limey liar."

As he spoke the words, he seemed completely sober, while at the same time he cracked the bottle against the door frame so that the jagged neck remained in his hand. Fighting Jack kicked his chair aside and stepped clear.

"Need a broken bottle, don't you, Indian? Can't face up t'a white man's fists." He disclosed just what one of these objects would look like by lifting up a clenched hand the size of a small spade. There was a crash as Sapper discarded the bottle and moved forward.

"Any white man can use his fists—but can one of them *Indian wrestle?*" The answer came in a roar.

"I can do anything you can do—but better!"

They stomped toward each other, feet shaking the building, while the men in between them fled. Not until they were standing face to face did they stop, noses touching, eyes glaring, teeth bared, like two bison muzzle to muzzle, or a pair of great locomotives neither of which would give way. With unspoken agreement they stepped sideways and sat at a recently emptied table, swept the glasses and bottles to the floor and hurled their coats from them, rolled up their sleeves and thudded their right elbows onto the scarred wood as they seated themselves. Their gazes locked as their hands met and grasped and squeezed, tight, each clenched tightly enough to crush solid wood but not tight enough to do any damage to the opposed member. With their grips strongly engaged, each man now exerted himself to push the other's hand back to the table so the knuckles touched, thereby winning. A simple enough procedure, easily and quickly resolved in most instances, as the stronger or more resolute man vanquished the other.

Not this time, however. If ever two giants were equally matched it was these two—and neither would give a fraction of an inch. The muscles in their arms stood out like gnarled steel and the tendons were bar-hard as every iota of strength they possessed went into the struggle. They were well matched, however, even too perfectly matched, for neither could gain an advantage, strain as he might. The crowd watched this battle of the titans with bulge-eyed attention, so silent with awe that when the muscles in Fighting Jack's upper arm split through his shirt the rip of the cloth could be clearly heard. A moment later the shirt across Sapper's brawny shoulders parted in the same manner from the strain. And still they fought on, locked in a rigid and deadly embrace: neither would give in, neither would relinquish victory.

There was a sharp crack as the top of the table split in two under their steady pressure and fell away. Now that their elbows were no longer supported they rose slowly to their feet, still locked equally, still straining with such force that it seemed human flesh and bone could not stand against it.

A whisper of awe susurrated through the room for it was scarcely believable, this sight which they were seeing with their own eyes. The hum and buzz of voices grew louder and there were a few cheers, including a war whoop from a table full of Onondagas. In response, one of the English navvies shouted out "Break him in half, Fighting Jack!" and there were other calls as well. Strangely enough, all of this had an odd effect on Sapper who, without relinquishing his hold in the slightest, looked up at his opponent and spoke, with some difficulty, so tightly cramped was his jaw.

"Are you . . . the head ganger . . . Fighting Jack?"

Fighting Jack had the same difficulty in speaking but managed to produce the words "I am."

The results of this simple statement were startling to say the least, for when he heard them Sapper ceased straining against the other's arm. Taken by surprise, Fighting Jack was off balance and fell sideways and was twisted around so that the Indian was able to slap him on the shoulder as he went by. The results were what might be expected, for the English ganger did not take lightly to this kind of treatment, so he continued turning until he had swung about in a full circle and was facing his opponent again—this time with his fists clenched and ready to do havoc. But before he could spring to the attack the Indian spoke.

"Well, I'm the head ganger, name of Sapper Cornplanter."

Fighting Jack's fists fell and he straightened up, evidencing the same look of surprise that had been on the other's face a few moments earlier. They faced each other like this, then began to smile, and in a moment began to laugh, shaking and bellowing with laughter to the bemusement and befuddlement of the onlookers, who were even more greatly shocked when the massive navvies clapped arms about each other's

151

shoulders, seized up bottles from the nearest tables, and went out of the door laughing and drinking together.

"I presume you could explain their actions," the Pinkerton man said.

"Surely" was Gus' response. "You know that Sapper is my head ganger here, and that Fighting Jack was my head ganger on the English end of the tunnel. Each man has heard of the other, knows of him by reputation, and knows as well that they are both my close friends, which to a navvy makes them butties as well. So you see they have no reason to fight but instead plenty of reason to drink together, which I am sure they are doing now."

As he finished speaking, Gus looked back to the table where the agent, Billygoat, was sitting, whom he had forgotten for the moment, and he fought hard to conceal the shock that overwhelmed him.

"He's gone! While we were watching the others, gone!"

Their mission was compromised; through inattention they had missed their chance to capture their saboteurs. Gus was abashed by this knowledge, but Tracy seemed coldly indifferent. He had his watch out, a large pocket turnip, and was looking at the face of it.

"While *you* were watching the others," said he coolly. "I am too much an old hand at these matters to be distracted that easily. During the excitement the contact man saw his opportunity and signaled to Billygoat, and they have both gone."

"You should have told me; now we will never find them."

"Quite the contrary; everything is going according to plan. I informed you that there were enemy watchers here, and if we had left right after the others, it would have been noticed and there would have been trouble. As it is, we can now pay for the slops we drank"—he threw some coins on the table as he said this—"and leave now that the excitement is over. We will not be followed." He glanced at his watch again before putting it away and climbing to his feet.

Gus came after, amazed at the other's calmness in the face of obvious disaster, following him down the dank passage and out into the street once again. They gained the mean avenue and Tracy turned in the direction of the waterfront.

"I will keep you in the darkness no longer, Washington," said he. "As you have technical secrets in your trade so do we in mine. And Pinkerton has the best. The agent, Billygoat, has a certain device concealed in his right boot, in reality built within the sole of the boot itself and indetectable by any normal search. When contact was made with him, he stamped his heel down hard in a precise manner. This ruptured a thin membrane within a cell that permitted acid in one half to flow into the other half, thereby transforming the inactive cell into an operating battery of great strength. The current thus generated goes to a powerful but compact radio generator also in the boot sole, the signal of which is sent up a wire that has been woven into the seam of his trousers. This connects to an aerial within his belt which broadcasts the powerful short-wave signal. You have seen me glancing at my watch?"

"I have indeed, and wondered at your sudden interest in the hour."

"Not the time at all, for this watch contains a compact receiver, a direction finder that is tuned to the radio signal from Billygoat. See for yourself."

He extracted the watch and held it flat in his hand, there being enough light from the nearest street gas lamp to make out the face. When he pressed the crown, the hour hand glowed softly and spun around to point down the street toward the sea; then it returned to its proper position indicating the correct time when he released his grip.

"Ingenious, wouldn't you agree? They are ahead of us, so let us proceed. We cannot see them, which is perfect, for that means they cannot see us and will be unalarmed. The radio will point the way."

As long as the street was well lit and occupied, they strolled along casually, just part of the throng. But when the avenue they were on ended at the unlighted docks, they turned around, as though completing a stroll there, and went back the way they had come. At the first turning they stopped for a moment and talked, still the casual strollers, while Tracy made sure they were not being observed. When they were clear he stepped into the shadows of the crossway and drew Gus after him.

153

"They are on the waterfront somewhere; the finder pointed in that direction. We shall make our way parallel to the harbor until we have a better indication of their destination."

They did this, stumbling over rubbish and litter and disturbing cats and rats in their nocturnal rounds, until Tracy halted once again at a crossing and studied the pointing hand.

"Most interesting, for it now points slightly back in the direction from whence we came. Washington, you are the engineer and the surveyor and have an eye for this sort of thing. Take a bearing here down the street, and we shall go back a bit to the next street for another cross bearing. Can you do that, determine where they are?"

"That is my trade," he said with some assurance, squinting along the tiny arrow.

When he had repeated this ritual, he thought for a moment, then led the Pinkerton agent forward to a spot where they could see the dark wharfs and the ships beyond. Unhesitatingly he pointed his finger.

"They are there."

"Aboard that ship? You are sure?"

"You said earlier that you could not be distracted from your job. I might say the same for mine."

"Then I unhesitatingly accept your information. We are ready for the final act to begin."

Tracy then moved back a few yards in the direction they had come from and raised a whistle to his lips and blew lustily into it. Gus was slightly startled when no sound, other than the slight hiss of escaping air, emerged from it. Tracy saw his expression of puzzlement and smiled.

"Supersonic sound, that is sound waves that are too high-pitched for the human ear to hear, but these sounds were not meant for the human ear, as you can see."

Two men appeared, the first of them leading a small dog on a leash. Tracy bent to pet the beast and explained. "Trained to come to that sound. These are my men who have been keeping watch over us waiting for my signal."

"I had no idea they were there."

"They are professionals."

Tracy issued swift orders, then he and Gus went forward once again. "My operators will surround the area and close in, but I must lead the attack. You need not come with me—"

"I am your man."

"Good. I was hoping you would. I want you there when the curtain falls on the last act of this little drama."

Tracy went first, silent as a cat, with Gus a few yards behind. They stayed close to the walls, in the darkness, and worked their way to the spot nearest the ship, where a single tiny lamp on deck cast a weak glow on the battered gangway. Tracy halted for a moment, looking at the ship, and when he did a shadow detached itself from the wall behind him and lurched forward.

Gus had only a split second to act in, and he did not want to call out a warning, so he jumped forward as well. His fist came up in a short, wicked arc that ended on the mysterious assailant's jaw with a sharp crack that caused Tracy to spin about. There was a small thud as the club the man had been wielding fell to the cobbles, then Tracy was helping Gus lower the unconscious man to the ground as well.

"I am glad you are here, Washington," said he, and from a man of his professional caliber this was reward enough. "That was a blow well struck and my men will have him before he regains consciousness. They will be closing in now to cut off all means of escape by the criminals, while fast launches will prevent flight by sea. The final act of this drama is about to be played. You were correct in your deductions, for I have checked my direction finder. Billygoat is aboard that ship. Now here we go."

Silent as a wraith he drifted forward, with Gus a few paces behind. They passed under the counter of the ship and her name could now be seen, picked out in rusty letters across the stern. *Der Liebestod, Lucerne.* Swiss registry, a flag of convenience obviously, with the real names and nationality of the true owners well concealed. But not much longer. All was silent on the deck above, the ship darkened except for that single bulb at the entranceway. Tracy walked forward steadily, as though he belonged here, and mounted the gangway, with Gus not too far behind. Yet, quiet as he was, he was not unobserved, for when he reached the deck a man stepped out of the shadows and mumbled something inaudible to Gus who was still on his way up. Tracy answered and pointed down and, as soon as the man had turned, the operative's hands struck and did something to the other's neck that kept him rigid for long moments before he folded and fell to the deck.

There was still no alarm, and Gus could not believe it. They had boarded the ship, rendered two men unconscious, and their presence was still unknown. Their luck seemed too good to last and he hoped that would not prove the case. Tracy waited in the open doorway until he came up, then whispered into his ear.

"The deckhouse is quiet and there is no one on the bridge—so the miscreants must be below. Follow me as silently as you are able."

With these words he pushed open the heavy iron door to disclose a dimly lit passageway beyond, into which he drifted. The first door off the passage was dark and he passed this opening with only a quick look, and the next, dark and open as well. But the one that followed was closed and he bent to peer through the keyhole, then took a doctor's stethoscope from his pocket and listened at the door panel with it. Satisfied, he restored it to his pocket and waved Gus on, pointing to the stairwell at the same time. Down this they went, slowly and carefully, and their reward was immediate, for one of the doors on this deck stood partly open and from it emerged a bar of light and a mutter of voices. Still leading, Tracy went forward, past another darkened doorway, with Gus close behind. As Gus passed the same doorway a dark figure, knife clutched in hand, leaped to the attack.

Only split-second reflexes saved his life. Gus fell back as the man hit him, falling under the swooping slice of the weapon, clutching at the knife arm, and rolling away with his assailant on top of him. There was a hearty thud as they fetched up against the bulkhead opposite, the force of the impact stunning the man for an instant, the force of Gus' fist stunning him more lastingly so that he sighed and went limp and the knife fell from his hand and rang loudly on the metal deck.

In the silence that followed the voice could be clearly heard through the open door.

"What was that? I heard something in the passageway."

Tracy stayed himself no longer. His revolver appeared in his hand, and as he kicked the door wide, he shouted defiantly, "This is the law and you are all under arrest!" then sprang into the room.

There were shouts, shots, muffled screams as Gus plunged forward, hurling himself without hesitation into the unknown fray, into a large cabin seemingly filled with rushing men. One of them tried to escape, but Gus was in his path and a hard fist in his middle bent him double, lowering his chin to the correct spot to connect with the other fist on its way up. Gus plunged on into the melee and raised his arm to prevent a blade from descending that was slashing at his throat and a red arrow of pain shot through his biceps as the blade cut deep. But he still had a good arm that ended in an equally good fist that dropped the attacker on the spot.

With that the battle was over, although Gus did not know it as he struggled to his feet, ignoring the pain of his wound. Disreputable men damaged in various ways lay sprawled about the room while Billygoat sat astride the single conscious survivor banging his head against the deck so that he could join his comrades in unconsciousness. Tracy moved quickly about, putting handcuffs on any that showed signs of life while Billygoat ceased his banging and rose, dusting off his hands and pointing at a closed door on the far side of the cabin.

"He went through there during the fracas. The Gray Man, the one in charge."

Tracy took in the situation in an instant and kicked a wicked-looking automatic pistol across to Billygoat who swooped it up.

"Guard the prisoners then because I want as many as possible alive."

Even as he spoke he was hurtling across the room to smash his shoulder into the flimsy connecting door, bursting through it with Gus, who had tied his kerchief about his wounded arm, right behind, straightening up and raising his gun and saying, "You will stop right there, for the jig is up."

The man he had addressed did stop what he was doing and straighten up slowly with a sheaf of papers in his hand. He had been thrusting these along with others of their kind into a metal wastebasket within which a smoky fire flared. As soon as Gus was aware of this, he leaped past the Pinkerton man and kicked the basket over to stomp out the smoldering flames. Only when this task was done did he straighten up and look at the man they had captured, the secret protagonist at last.

He was indeed a gray man as Billygoat had said. He stood erect beside the desk there, one fist pressed to it, the other to his chest, swaying slightly. From toe to top he was gray, clad completely in gray from the gray spats that covered his gray shoes, gray trousers, and gray suit, of a good cut, gray broadcloth shirt with matching gray tie, a gray fedora upon his head and a mask of gray cloth that concealed his face except for the pair of holes cut in the fabric through which peered a pair of gray eyes.

"Do not make a move," Tracy ordered as the man's hand moved toward the desk. The gray man jerked back his hand and responded in a strained whisper.

"There is money in the drawer here, much money to pay those outside. It is all yours, thousands of pounds. All you must do is turn your back for a few moments, that is all, I beg of you. Let me leave—"

"You take me for a fool, sir! I am of the Pinkertons and in the employ of The Transatlantic Tunnel Company, and there is no bribe in the world big enough to tempt me to compromise my honor. You are taken and that is the end of it. The game is up."

At this the gray man crumpled in such a tragic manner that Gus was tempted to go to his aid. All semblance of power was gone now and the figure trembled, groping behind for a chair to drop into. The professional Pinkerton operator was as unaffected as Gus was touched, for he had apprehended many a hardened criminal before, so that when he spoke it was harshly.

"Now sir, you will remove that mask—or shall we do it for you?"

"No . . . please, no . . ." was the gasped answer, but it touched Tracy not. Gun held at the ready, he stepped forward, seized mask and hat in one hand, and with a single gesture hurled them aside. Gus gasped.

Sitting there, the mask removed, was someone he knew, someone he would never have suspected, someone who could not possibly be in this place at this time.

"Do you know who that is?" asked he.

"A hardened criminal," Tracy responded.

"No, it can't be, he is not. But still he is here. It is unbelievable."

"You know him then?"

"Of course I do! That is none other than Henry Stratton, a respected financier from Boston and a member of the New York branch of The Transatlantic Tunnel Board of Directors."

"Well then, it seems we have our man at last. A member of the board of directors indeed! It is no wonder the criminals were privy to all your secrets and could strike wherever they wished."

While they spoke, Stratton sat with lowered eyes, limp with exhaustion and defeat, uncaring. However, when they had finished, he struggled to bring himself erect, and a little of his old fire returned to his voice that no longer whispered.

"I beg of you gentlemen to release me. The disgrace, my family, you cannot understand. If I am released I promise. . . ."

"No," said Tracy and in his word was the immutability of doom, the monolithic force of destiny, so powerful that Stratton wilted again under the irresistible assault.

"Yes, you are right, I should not ask, a last desperate attempt of a desperate man. I am doomed and have been so since the beginning had I but the wit to realize it."

"But why?" Gus burst out. "What could lead you, a respected member of the community, to such reprehensible actions?"

Stratton looked up at him slowly, then smiled a wintry smile that held no slightest touch of humor.

"Why? I might have expected you to ask that kind of question, Washington, since you are the sort that is never bothered by the kind of human problems that trouble others.

You are a machine for building tunnels, that is what you are, and do not suffer from the frailties of us mortals. You ask why? I will tell you and it is a sordid story indeed, a progress into hell that began with but one false step. I am a member of the board and have invested my all in the company. But I was greedy and wished more, so secretly sold some stock from an estate for which I am executor to buy more tunnel stock, meaning to return the money as soon as the first dividends were paid. But these were stocks in a certain shipping company, for mine is a family with old shipping interests, and I never knew that I was being closely watched. I was approached by—shall we say, parties in the shipping business—who knew everything I had done. They promised to help me, and they did, so my thefts would not be discovered, and I had but to render them certain small services in return. I did these things, acting as a spy within the board for them, passing on information until I was too compromised to back out. Then they pressed for more and more services until I ended up where you see me now; on the one hand, a respected member of the board, while, on the other, I direct the secret agency that is doing its best to destroy the tunnel. Gad! I am glad it is at an end at last."

"Who are these people who have done this to you?" asked Gus.

Stratton waved a weary hand in the direction of the papers scattered around the cabin.

"It is all there; you will find out for yourself soon enough. Shipping interests, foreign countries, all the men of power and men of evil who felt that the tunnel would do them no good, the countries who wish England and the empire ill-will at all times. A consortium of crime such as has never been seen before. It is all there, my correspondence, carbon copies, notes, directives, every bit of it, for I am a thoroughly organized and efficient New England businessman, and whatever business I transact, no matter how low, is done in a meticulous manner. All you need is here. With it you will be able to destroy the ring and the saboteurs forever; you have my word on that. It will all come out, I can see that now, and my good name will be ruined forever. Therefore, I ask you but one favor. Gather up the papers and quit this room for a few minutes. I will not be long. There is only the single tiny porthole so you know I cannot escape in that manner. Please, I beg of you, as men of honor."

"No," said Tracy firmly, "for you are our best witness."

"Yes," said Washington with the voice of command. "We have prisoners enough outside, if it is prisoners that you are interested in. What I care about is stopping the sabotage and exposing the fiends who are behind it—and we have them here in these papers. Look at these names! Respected men, powerful companies! There will be arrests and some sliding stocks in the market, and the sabotage will end once and for all. The foreign governments can't be touched, but their active interests can be exposed and that will keep them in line for a good while. We have what we need here. I insist that we grant Mr. Stratton's request."

Tracy hesitated a moment, then shrugged. "Justice will be served and my fee will be just the same. If you insist—and take full responsibility for the decision."

"I do. And I know Sir Winthrop will back me up."

As they gathered up the papers and prepared to leave, the voice of the ruined man hissed after them. "I hate you, Washington, you and all the things you stand for. But, for my family's sake, I begrudgingly offer thanks."

Soon after the door was closed behind them a single shot broke the stillness and after that all was silent again.

III. DANGER IN THE DEEPS

Here, two miles beneath the surface of the Atlantic, was the realm of eternal night; dark, silent, and still, an empty world of black water. The surface of the ocean with its winds and weather, breaking waves, surging currents and burgeoning life was more than 10,000 feet above. That was where the sunlight was and the plankton, the microscopic life forms that cannot live without it, and the small fish that graze upon these seagoing meadows, and the larger fish that feed upon them in turn. Up there was the sun with its energy and the oxygen that made life possible in the ocean depths, and just as the depth increases so does the quantity of life decrease until, a mile down, the tiny piscine monsters who dwell at this dark level are few and far between. Strange creatures of needle teeth and bulging eyes, with rows of lights like portholes down their sides or hanging out in front, tiny mites of ferocity like *Chiasmodon niger,* just two inches long but so voracious it swallows fish bigger than itself. But this was the last battleground, for below there was little life and less motion, until the bottom was reached at a depth of three miles where a great current flows in the direction opposite to the Canary Current on the surface above. But here it was black, empty, lifeless, still, unchanging.

Yet, can it be, is that *something* approaching far in the distance? Lights, yes, indeed, lights, pinpoints of brightness in the endless night, moving steadily along. A school of fish perhaps, for the lights grow more and more numerous until they stretch away and dim out of sight. Wait, there seem to be two different species here, smaller fish, though small only in comparison, for they are as big as blue whales, surrounding an immense sea snake that undulates through the water with serpentine skill, a snake with its own rows of lights down its sides that go on and on, an incredible creature that is over a mile in length. But what is this?—the snake is held captive by the smaller fish, linked to them with strong bonds, pulled along by them. What manner of creatures are these with hard, smooth skins, eyeless yet with burning lights, humming and thrashing loudly as they disturb the stillness of the deeps? No living beast at all, but metal shells containing the only living creature that dares to enter this lifeless realm, man, the most daring animal of all.

Ahead of all the other submarines was the *Nautilus II,* far mightier and more complex than her atomized namesake, with a crew of thirty needed to manage all the machines and devices she contained. Few of them were needed to control the submarine, for she was as simple to operate as her predecessor, but were there instead to manipulate the ancillary apparatus. Steel cables ran from reels set into her keel, stretching out to the front of the mile-long tow, controlled by automatic devices that monitored these cables constantly, keeping them at a certain tension, letting out a length of cable when the pressure rose to high, reeling in some when it dropped. The information about the tension on the cables was fed along electric wires to an enormous Brabbage computer engine that took up almost a quarter of the space in the submarine, that received information from the cables of every other one of the submarines as well, monitoring them all, adjusting tension and pull so they moved as one with their immense burden. No material wires connected the engine to the other submarines; communication was carried on by immaterial wires of another sort—beams of light, coherent light from the numerous lasers that studded the hulls. These laser beams penetrated the water with ease, and their energies were modulated to carry the needed information. All went well, all worked well, a tribute to the innate ingenuity of man that had conceived this project in the first place, of which this was the final section. From New York City the train tracks now sped, to dive under the waters and rush across the ocean floor in the newly manufactured tunnel there to enter the fracture zone that split the ocean bed, to rise up through this into the mountains of the Mid-Atlantic Ridge where they ended at the very tip of the canyon that bisected this ridge. On the far side of the Atlantic a similar length of track left London and entered the tunnel there and moved out to the Azores, to lift up briefly before diving again to the abyssal plain, reaching next the fracture zone and the opposite edge of the canyon. There the two tunnels ended, their blank ends facing each other across a mile of empty water at the very edge of the Rift Valley depths that plunged far out of sight below.

Here now, at last, swimming slowly to its destiny, came the incredible sea snake of the mile-long tunnel that was both tunnel and bridge, an upside-down bridge that floated, that would pull *up* against its supports instead of hanging down, a steel and concrete, cunningly contrived bridge-tunnel that did indeed undulate like a snake as it swam along. The secret of its motion was the joints between sections, bellowslike constructions of solid steel, steel strong enough to resist the great pressures of the deeps, yet flexible enough to bend as needed. This was the mighty construction that would finish the Herculean labor at last, this was the final link in the tunnel between the continents. It had been two long years in the building, the sections constructed at different sites and floated to the rendezvous up the Hudson River, below the ruined fortress of West Point, long associated with the heroic General Benedict Arnold. Here a new form of warfare was engaged; man against the elements, battling to conquer the endless sea. Section by section the bridge-tunnel had been joined together and tested until the incredible structure was completed. Then, on the ebb of the tide, it had been submerged and floated down to the sea, the beginning of the journey that was now reaching its final stages.

On the bridge, O'Toole sat at the controls, or rather watched the controls, because the computer set the course for this submarine as well.

"There are some things that take a bit of getting used to," said he, arms folded so his fingers wouldn't twitch toward the levers and buttons, eyeing the compass suspiciously as it swung a bit then steadied. "Now I know in theory that we are homing in on the sonar beacon at the bridge site, and that the infernal machine back in the bilges is pointing us all that way and running the engines and the rest, now I *know* that, but sure and I do not *believe* it."

"I think you do," Gus said, smiling as he bent over the plotting table and noted their slow but steady progress across the map. "All you want is a little action, a fist fight or a few drinks or something like that."

"How you blacken the name of O'Toole!" he cried, with no sincerity at all, but with a matching smile as well. "Though truth be known a jar of Guinness would not be refused, I'm thinking."

A light glowed red on the board and his fingers rushed to the controls and made certain adjustments. "Proximity to beacon ten miles, dead ahead."

"Time to begin cutting our speed. We want to be at almost zero forward motion when we reach the canyon so we can use our maneuverability against the current." He called down to the computer section and issued the needed commands.

Slower and slower the great snake drifted, taking many miles to slow down, so great was its mass. The sonar beacons, strategically placed below, guided it to the correct spot where all forward motion ceased, where the final drop could begin. One mile straight down, out of the still waters into the bottom current which, slow moving as it was, still exerted a powerful force on anything as massive as this bridge-tunnel. The flow of the current had been carefully measured and this was one of the factors that was also taken into consideration by the computer so that when the bridge began the drop of the last mile it was still some miles upstream from the tunnel site. As the giant construction fell at a regular rate it would be carried along at a certain speed as well, theoretically to end up at the correct spot at the correct depth.

The last fall began. Delicate pressure mechanisms in each tunnel section admitted sea water to the ballast tanks as they drifted downwards so that while the pressure increased the tunnel always had the same slight positive buoyancy. Down and down and down—until at last ruddy lights were visible below and the computer had the laser beams as more definite navigation points. It digested this new information instantly, and some of the submarines went faster while others slowed so the bridge bent and straightened again as it was turned slightly and aligned with the still invisible piers in the depths.

"There they are," Gus said, pointing at the lights now visible on the television screen of the darkened bridge, television because the egg-shaped, thick-walled submarines that operated at these depths dared not have openings or ports of any kind in their hulls, so that all outside viewing was done by electronic means, with pickups at bow and stern, topside and in the keel. It was the keel pickup that now revealed the lights below and ahead of them. "We are on course to five decimal places," said he, looking at the readout from the computer beside him.

Now the final, most delicate and most dangerous part of the mission was about to begin. The current here flowed steadily and smoothly at a speed of almost one and a half knots, hardly anything to speak of; if it had been on the surface, a good swimmer could have breasted it, a rowing boat made progress in it, a fast launch ignored it. Even below the sea the submarines paid the current scarcely any heed—when they were on their own. But now, with their massive tow, it became their primary consideration, for the thirty-foot-thick and mile-long bridge had an immense surface area that the current pushed against, so strongly that it was doubtful if the united force of all the submarines could have held it steady, much less gained against its pull. Therefore the attempt to put the bridge sections into place must be right the very first time.

In order to accomplish this the cables had to be secured on each side of the valley at the same time and locked into place. The towing lines from the submarines were fastened to the much more massive cables of the bridge, each over a yard in diameter, for these served a dual function, now being used for towing, but upon arrival they would become the permanent mooring cables that held the bridge in the correct position. The ones from the center section were the longest— well over a half mile in length because they had to connect to the buttresses at each end—while the others grew shorter and shorter the closer they came to the end. When in position, this skein of steel cables would hold the bridge inflexibly in place as its buoyancy pulled them taut. Now it was a matter of securing them.

Below the lip of each edge of the canyon there was a great area of smoothed rock that was illuminated brilliantly by numerous lights, for what had to be done next had to be done by eye, the human eye, and no automatic machines could be of aid here. Massive, monstrous anchors had been drilled and cemented into the solid stone to hold the bridge in place, while secured to them were hulking fittings to which would eventually be attached the giant turnbuckles that would be used to tension the cables correctly. But that would come later; now the cables had to be secured quickly and easily. In order to do this, massive, spring-loaded, forged steel jaws projected from each anchor. When a cable was pressed across one of these sets of jaws, they would be sprung like a titanic rat trap and would snap shut instantly, their corrugated jaws latching fast while automatic electric motors tightened them even more. This was the plan and it had been tested many times in training and it should work. It *must* work!

Down, down, down, the massive construction fell, with its attentive tugs laboring hard, now pulling this way, now that, under the continuous instruction of the Brabbage engine. There was almost complete silence inside the submarines, aside from the whisper from the ventilation louvers and the distant hum of the engines, an occasional word spoken between the operators of the great computer. Despite the silence and the lack of activity the air of tension was so thick inside every one of the subs that there were those who had some difficulty in breathing, for this was it, the irreversible decision, the unchangeable moment.

Down steadily while the brightly lit anchors below grew larger on the screens, the bold red numbers above each of them standing out stark and clear, and down still more with the cliff coming closer and closer. Fists tightened and knuckles whitened as the pilots simply watched their charges control themselves under the tutelage of the computer brain, this waiting and watching infinitely more trying than any complex control effort would have been. Down. Every detail of the ancient stone and the clean sharpness of the new construction clear before them. Down.

"One and nine attach, one and nine attach. You are on your own!"

The voice spoke quickly and clearly over the command circuits, booming from every speaker in every sub. This was the long-awaited signal, manual command, the first subs on their way with their cables. Ten cables at each end of the bridge, numbers one and two being the shortest on top of the pier, nine and ten the longest because, from the center of the span, their cables had to reach far down to the bottom of the pier. Now the two subs each with one of the pair of the longest and shortest cables had been released from computer command and were moving ahead on their own to attach their cables, racing at full speed to make their hookups. As soon as they had done this the next two subs would be sent in with their cables during the vital two minutes during which the tunnel would be in the right place at the right distance for hookup. That is all that was needed, four cables on each end to anchor the bridge-tunnel against the pressure of the current. If these eight cables were secured, the bridge would be held in place; the computations had been exact. Once these eight were in place the remaining mooring cables would be attached one at a time with greater precision. But those four cables had to be fastened first; if they were not, there was no telling what disaster might occur as the bridge was swept out of position.

Nautilus II, motors whining at full speed, led the way toward the anchorage, O'Toole busy at last with the controls, yet even as he dived, remembering to ease off on the keel line and tighten up on the bow line that was fastened to the mooring cable like a spring, riding loosely until now. The drum and motor for this line were on a spar that jutted twenty feet from the sub's nose and were easily visible in the forward camera. Well before the sub had reached its goal the heavy mooring cable had been reeled in until it was snug against the end of the spar, the orange-painted twenty-foot-long section of cable just above it. This was the target area.

As long as any portion of this colored area was snagged by the waiting jaws the hookup would be successful, for this area was well within the bending tolerances of the bridge and the natural arc of the cable. For precise measurements a two-foot-wide black band was painted about the middle of the orange section, the area of optimum choice.

O'Toole handled the bulky submarine with an artist's touch, spinning it on its beam ends so the spar pointed up and out at the waiting jaws, taking up the weight of the cable, being forced astern for a moment, then thrusting out—but not so fast that he rammed the pier. Up slowly, drifting, correcting, forward, the spar like an immense guiding finger reaching out for the target. Gus, standing behind the pilot, unconsciously held his breath as the pier moved closer and closer until it seemed they would ram into it.

"Got it!" O'Toole shouted with joy as the iron jaws, like a great metal alligator, slammed crunching shut on the cable just on the black band, so strongly they could feel the impact within the submarine. "And now clear and we're away."

He pressed the two buttons that sent an electric current through the wires inside the towing lines, a current which exploded the shackles that secured them to the anchoring cables. The smaller lines dropped free and the electric motors whined to run them in as the submarine backed away.

"Number nine hooked as well," Gus said, looking at the scene from the keel pickup on his monitor screen. "Numbers two and ten begin approach," he ordered into the command circuit.

At that precise moment it happened, just then at the worst possible time for the anchoring of the bridge, a moment when success and failure were suspended on a razor edge of seconds. But world time is a measurement on a different scale; rather say that geologic time is indifferent to mankind's brief existence on the outer skin of the globe, experiencing thousands of years or even hundreds of thousands of years as the smallest unit. Pressures had been building in the Earth's core as the tidal flow of molten rock pressed up against the solid crust that floated upon it, building pressure slowly but insistently, pressure that had to be relieved for it could not be endured too long. A seam deep in the rocks opened, a great mass shifted, stone grated on stone and the pressures were equalized, the Earth was at rest again. A small thing in geological time, too small to be even measured or noticed in comparison to the mighty forces always at work. Yet large enough to wreak havoc to man's work.

Inside the solid Earth there was a deep grumbling as of some immense giant complaining and turning in his sleep, a sound so great it shook the solid stone above and transmitted itself to the water which in turn struck the solid steel fabric of the submarines, jarring them and tossing them about before passing on.

"Earthquake . . ." Gus said, rising from the deck where he had been thrown, "an undersea quake, just now. . . ."

He stopped, aghast at what was happening outside, the scene so clearly displayed on the screen. The tremors in the Earth had been passed to the anchored cables which were bending and writhing like things alive, sending traveling shock waves along their length to the lightly anchored bridge above. The bridge and anchoring cables had been designed to absorb shocks and quakes like these, but as a unit, well secured and soundly anchored. Now the two cables were bearing all the strain that twenty had been designed for. It was impossible; it was happening. What damage was being wrought to the bridge! Gus dared not stop to consider; the damage before his eyes was even greater, for harshly burdened and overstrained, the cables were tearing from their fittings.

Terrible to see, impossible to turn away from, the heavy steel and concrete anchors crumbling and shattering, breaking free. Pulling from the moment's paralysis, Gus grabbed for the communicator.

"Number two, draw back or release your cable, do you hear me?"

"I can attach, I can—"

The words cut off, never finished as tragedy struck. With the two holding cables torn loose, the floating bridge above twisted and moved, bent, floating free, dragging on the attached cables. The submarine, number two that was about to attach its cable, was simply lashed forward like a child's toy at the end of a string and thrown against the stony wall. It took a fraction of an instant, no more, as the pressure hull cracked and the incredible weight of the water at this depth compressed, destroyed, flattened the vessel in the smallest part of a second, so quickly that her crew must have had no slightest warning of their doom. It fell slowly, a dead weight at the end of the cable.

Gus could spend no time with concern for the dead now, for he must think of the living, the submarines still attached to the bridge and the fate of the bridge itself. For long seconds he forced himself to stand there, to think logically, to consider every factor before going into action, while all the time the communicator roared with voices, questions, cries of anguish. Reaching a decision, he smashed down the command switch and spoke with cold clarity into the microphone.

"Clear all communication circuits, silence, absolute silence, this is Washington speaking and I want silence." And he received it, for within seconds the last voice died away and as soon as it had he spoke again. "Come in, second-section commander, give a report. We have had a quake at this end and are not connected. What is your condition." The response was immediate.

"Section two commander here. All in the green. Four cables connected, about to go for the next two. Some tremors and movement apparent on our lines."

"Connect next two then suspend operations. Hold at your end for future orders. Attention all first-section subs. We have broken free here and cannot reconnect until bridge is in correct mode. Orders for all odd-numbered subs, all odd-numbered subs, activate your disconnect charges from cables now and proceed south, away from the bridge until out of the area of free cables, then return *over* the bridge, repeat, over. There will be loose cables below. Commands now for even-numbered subs. Turn north at once and into the current, full power ahead, rise at same time to level of the bridge. Execute."

It was a desperate maneuver, a plan conceived in a few moments in an attempt to master this unforeseen situation, a complicated stratagem that had to be enacted faultlessly in the midnight deeps where every man and every sub was separate and alone, yet interdependent. In his mind's eye Gus could see the bridge and he went over what must be done again in detail and was convinced that he was attempting the only thing possible.

The floating bridge was secured to its pier at one end only, the opposite end on the eastern cliff. With the west end unattached, the current would push against the structure, bending it down-current to the south, bending it more and more until it broke and water flooded the air-filled tunnel sections, robbing it of its buoyancy so it would hang downward, fracturing and being destroyed along its entire length. This could not happen! The first thing he had to do was detach all the odd-numbered subs which, like his own vehicle, had been towing the bridge from the southern, down-current, side. If any attempt was made to pull on the bridge with these cable moorings from the up-current side, they would twist the bridge as though trying to wind it up and this would destroy it as quickly as the current. If all was going correctly, the odd-numbered subs would have released their cables by now and would be fleeing up over the bridge; *Nautilus II* was below the freed cables so she could swing up-current and rise to join the subs that remained attached to their mooring cables. These would be fighting to keep the bridge from bending, pulling in a northerly direction with the full power of their engines. Pray they would succeed!

As the *Nautilus II* churned upwards they saw a horrifying sight on their screens, the view from their topside pickup. The row of lights on the bridge was no longer a straight line, but had curved instead into a monstrous letter *C* where the free end was being swept south by the current. Gus took one look, then snapped on the command circuit.

"To all subs who have dropped their cables. Rejoin others above who are attempting to hold the position of the west end of the bridge, use your magnetic grapples to secure to these subs, then use full reverse power as well. We *must* stop the bridge from bending; we must straighten it."

Nautilus II led the way, nuzzling up beside one of the straining subs, touching her, then being held fast as the powerful electromagnet on the hull seized tight to the other. As soon as they were attached, the engines whined, louder and louder, as they sped up to full reverse revolutions. If this helped, it was not immediately visible, for the bridge bent and bent even more until the free end was pointing almost due south. The designers had allowed for flexibility, but certainly not for this much; it would surely break at any moment.

Yet it did not. One by one the other subs latched onto their mates and added their power to the total effort. They could not straighten out the frightening bend, but it appeared they had it checked at last. They were not gaining, but at least they had stopped losing. They needed more power.

"Attention all units of section two. Continue attaching cables your end. We are barely holding here. As each unit secures its cable, proceed at maximum speed to this end and grapple to another sub. We need your help."

It came. One after another the other submarines swam up out of the darkness and ran their hulls against the subs already there until they clustered together like grapes, two, three, and four in a group, straining at the cables. At first there seemed to be no result, try as hard as they could, then—was it happening?—was the curve shallower? It was almost impossible to tell. Gus rubbed at his eyes as O'Toole spoke.

"Sure and I'm not the one to be making empty claims, but it's my feeling that we're moving astern just the smallest amount." No sooner were the words from his mouth than the communicator buzzed.

"*Anemone* here. I am in position near the cliff face and have been observing. Southern motion stopped. We appear now to be moving north at a very slow but steady pace."

"Thank you, *Anemone*," said Gus. "Well done. Can you hear me, *Periwinkle?*"

"*Periwinkle* here."

"You have the heavy grappling equipment. Proceed up to the free section of the bridge and locate the second cable on the southern side. Repeat, second cable, labeled *number three*. The first cable was anchored but tore free. Follow this cable down to the orange marker, grapple there and attempt to attach to mounting number three. Do you understand?"

"I'm on my way."

Pulling mightily, engines flat out, the reluctant bridge was

173

dragged against the current until it was in the correct position, to be held there while *Periwinkle* grappled cable after hanging cable and attached them. Only when all the down-current cables had been attached did Gus allow the cables they were tugging at to be grappled and put in position. As soon as the first one was down and secured, he permitted himself to relax, to draw in a deep shuddering breath.

"One crew, one sub destroyed," he said to himself as memory returned after the endless period of effort. He was not aware of O'Toole and the others looking at him with something resembling awe, nodding agreement when O'Toole spoke for them all.

"You did it, Captain Washington, you did it despite the quake. No one else could have—but you did it. Good men died, but no one could have prevented that. Still the bridge is in place and no more casualties. You did it!"

IV. THE END OF THE EXPERIMENT

"You are through to Sunningdale," the club porter said. "If you will take it in the telephone room, sir."

Washington nodded and hurried to the glass-doored chamber with its leather armchair and brocade walls. The loudspeaker was built into the wings of the chair by his head, the switch at his fingertips in the arm, the microphone before his lips. He sat and threw the switch on.

"Are you there? Washington speaking."

"Gus, is that you? How nice of you to call. Where are you?"

"At my club, London. Joyce, I wonder, could I ask a favor of you?"

He had met Joyce Boardman a number of times, taking her to lunch in London when he was in town, for she still saw a good deal of Iris. Joyce, happily married, knew how sorely he was troubled and without his asking told him all she knew of Iris, all that had transpired since last they had met. It was small solace, but it was something, and both of them enjoyed these luncheons though the real reason for their meetings was never mentioned. Now there was silence for a moment on the line before Joyce answered, since he had asked nothing of her before.

"But of course, anything within reason, you know that."

Now it was Gus' turn for silence, for he felt a certain embarrassment in speaking his mind like this; he clenched his fist hard. He had to say it.

"It's a, well, personal matter, as I am sure you have guessed. You read the papers, so you know that the tunnel is just about completed; in fact, I am in London for the final arrangements. I leave in the morning for New York, which

175

should wind things up, the opening train coming up and all that, but pretty well finished here. What I would like, I cannot do it directly, I wonder—if you could arrange a meeting with Iris."

He brought the words out in a rush and sat back; he had said it. Joyce laughed and he felt the flush rising in his face before she hurried to explain.

"Excuse me, please, I was laughing, you know, because of the coincidence, just too uncanny. Do you remember that first night we met, at the Albert Hall?"

"I am sure I will never forget it."

"Yes, I realize, but there was this speaker there, the philosopher and scientist Dr. Judah Mendoza, the one with all the time theories, really fascinating indeed. I've been to all his lectures, sometimes with Iris, and this afternoon he will be at my home, a small soirée, along with the medium Madame Clotilda. She doesn't work well before large audiences so this has been arranged. Just a few people. You're welcome to come of course. Two o'clock. Iris will be here as well."

"The perfect thing, I'll be ever grateful."

"Tush. I can count on you then?"

"You could not keep me away!"

Gus saw nothing outside during the cab ride and the short train trip into the countryside, for his eyes were looking inward. What could he do? What could he say? Their futures were in the hands of Sir Isambard, and at that morning's meeting he had seemed as crusty as ever, even with the tunnel finished. Could he possibly change? *Would* he change? There were no easy answers.

It was a kindly summer day, the old houses on each side of the curving street surrounded by a wealth of colorful blossoms replete with bees droning about with their burdens of nectar. Weathered wood, russet tiles, green lawns, blue sky, a perfect day, and Gus drew heart. With the world as peaceful as this, the tunnel almost done, there must be an understanding between them. Too many years of sacrifice had gone by already; there had to be an end to it.

A maid showed him in when he rang and Joyce, in a

floor-sweeping dress, came to take his hand. "Iris will be here at any moment—come and meet the others."

The others were mostly women, none of whom he knew, and he mumbled his hellos. There were two men, one of them a bearded professor of some sort who had crumbs of food on his lapels, a thick German accent, and bad breath. Gus quickly took his sherry and seated himself by the other man, also an academic but one at least of whom he had heard, Reverend Aldiss, the warden of All Souls. The warden, a tall, erect man with an impressive nose and jaw, was having no trifle with sherry but instead held a large whisky in his hand. For a moment Gus wondered what he was doing here, then remembered that in addition to his college work the warden had no small literary reputation as the author of a number of popular scientific romances under the *nom de plume* of Argentmount Brown. These parallel world theories were undoubtedly meat and drink to him. They talked a bit, for the warden had a keen interest in the tunnel and a knowledge of the technical problems involved, and listened closely and nodded while Gus explained. This ended when Iris came in; Gus excused himself abruptly and went over to her.

"You are looking very good," said he, which was only the truth, for the delicate crow's-feet in the corners of her eyes made her more attractive if anything.

"And you, keeping well? The tunnel is approaching completion, father tells me. I can't begin to explain how proud I am."

They could say no more in this public place, though her eyes spoke a deeper message, one of longing, of solitary days and empty nights. He understood and they both knew that nothing had changed between them. There was time only for a few more polite words before they were all called in; the séance was about to begin. The curtains had been drawn shut so that only a half light filtered into the room. They sat in a semicircle facing Dr. Mendoza who stood with his back to the fireplace, hands under coattails, as though seeking warmth from the cold hearth, while beside him the rotund Madame Clotilda lay composed upon the sofa. Mendoza coughed loudly until he had absolute silence, patted his skullcap as though to make sure it was in place, stroked his full gray beard, which indubitably was still there, and began.

"I see among us this day some familiar faces as well as some I do not know, so I venture to explain some of the few things we have uncovered in our serious delving. There is but a single alpha-node that has such a weight of importance that it overwhelms all others in relation to this world as we know it, and to the other world we have been attempting to explore, which is our world, one might say, as we do *not* know it. This alpha-node is the miserable shepherd Martin Alhaja Gontran, killed in 1212. In this other world we examine, which I call Alpha Two, ours of course being Alpha One, the shepherd lived and the Moors did not win the battle of Navas de Tolosa. A Christian country by the name of Spain came into existence in the part of the Iberian Peninsula we know as the Iberian Caliphate, along with a smaller Christian country called Portugal. Events accelerate, these brawling, lusty new countries expand, send settlers to the new worlds, fight wars there, the face of the globe changes. We look back to England for a moment, since this is the question asked me most often, what of England? Where were we? Did not John Cabot discover North and South America? Where are our brave men? The answer seems to lie in this world of Alpha Two with a debilitating English civil war called, oddly enough, we cannot be sure of all details, the War of the Tulips, though perhaps not, Madame Clotilda was unsure, England not being Holland, perhaps War of the Roses would be more exact. England's substance was spent on internal warfare, King Louis the Eleventh of France living to old age, involved in English wars constantly."

"Louis died of the pox at nineteen," Warden Aldiss muttered. "Good thing, too." Doctor Mendoza blew his nose on a kerchief and went on.

"Much is not explained and today I hope we will clear up some of the difficulties, for I will attempt to forget history and all those strange Spanish-speaking Aztecs and Incas, most confusing indeed, and we will try to describe the world of

Alpha Two as it is today, this year, now. Madame, if you please."

They looked on quietly as Dr. Mendoza made the elaborate passes and spoke the incantations that put the medium into her trance. Madame Clotilda sank into an easy sleep, hands clasped on her mountainous bosom, breathing smoothly and deeply. But when the doctor attempted to bring her into contact with the Alpha-2 world, she protested, though still remaining unconscious, her body twitching and jiggling, her head tossing this way and that. He was firm in his endeavors and permitted no digressing so that in the end his will conquered hers and she acquiesced.

"Speak," he commanded, and the order could not be disobeyed. "You are there now in this world we know and spoke of, you can see it about you, tell us of it, tell us of England, the world, the colonies, speak, tell us, inform us, for we want to hear. *Speak!*"

She spoke, first rambling words, out of context perhaps, nonsense syllables, then clearly she described what never had been.

"Urhhh . . . urrhhh . . . penicillin, petrochemicals, purchase tax . . . income tax, sales tax, anthrax . . . Woolworth's, Marks & Sparks . . . great ships in the air, great cities on the ground, people everywhere. I see London, I see Paris, I see New York, I see Moscow, I see strange things. I see armies, warfare, killing, tons, tons, tons, tons of bombs from the air on cities and people below, hate him, kill him, poison gas, germ warfare, napalm, bomb, big bombs, atom bombs, hydrogen bombs, bombs dropping, men fighting killing dying, hating, it is, it is . . . ARRRRRGH!"

She ended with a scream and her body flopped about like a great rag doll tossed by some invisible beast. Gus rushed forward to help, but Dr. Mendoza waved him away as a doctor appeared from the kitchen where he had been waiting, undoubtedly in case of a seizure like this. Gus went back to his chair and saw a startled face appear in the doorway behind. The master of the house, Tom Boardman, whom he had met once, took one wild-eyed look at the incredible scene in his drawing room, then fled upstairs. Mendoza was speaking again, mopping his face at the same time with his bandanna.

"We can hear no more, Madame will not approach this area, she cannot stand it, as we can see why instantly. Such terrible nightmare forces. Hearing of it, we are forced to some reluctant conclusions. Perhaps this world does not exist after all, for it sounds terrible and we cannot possibly imagine how it could have become like that, so perhaps it is just the weird imaginings of the medium's subconscious mind, something we must always watch for in these investigations. We will pursue the matter deeper, if we can, but there seems little hope of success, of possibly contacting this world as I once hoped to. A false hope. We should be satisfied with our own world, imperfect as it may be."

"Are there no more details of it?" Warden Aldiss asked.

"Some, I can supply them if you wish. Perhaps they are more suitable for a scientific romance than for reality. I for one would not enjoy living in the world so described."

There were murmurs of assent from all sides of the room, and Gus took the opportunity to take Iris' hand and lead her from the room, through the French windows and into the garden. They walked under the apple trees, already heavy with fruit, and he banished the memory of the recent strange experience from his mind and spoke of the matter closest to his heart.

"Will you marry me, Iris?"

"Would that I could! But—"

"Your father?"

"He is still an ill man; he works too hard. He needs me. Perhaps when the tunnel is done, I'll take him away somewhere, make him retire."

"I doubt if he will ever do that."

She nodded agreement and shook her head helplessly, turning to take both his hands in hers. "I am afraid that I doubt it, too. Gus, dear Gus, is there to be no future for us after all these years of waiting?"

"There has to be. I will talk to him after the inaugural run.

With the tunnel completed, our differences should no longer count."

"They will still count with father. He is a stern man."

"You would not leave him to marry me?"

"I cannot. I cannot seek my own happiness by injuring another."

His logical mind agreed with her, and he loved her even the more for her words. But in his heart he could not bear the answer that would keep them apart. Torn, unhappy, they reached out and clasped hands tightly and looked deep into each other's eyes. There were no tears in Iris' eyes this time, perhaps because they had been shed all too often before. A cloud crossed the sun and darkness fell across them and touched deep into their hearts as well.

V. THE WONDERFUL DAY

What a day, what a glorious day to be alive! Children present on this day would grow old with memories they would never forget, to sit by the fire some future evening and tell other wide-eyed children, yet unborn, about the wonder of this day. A cheerful sun shone brightly on City Hall Park in New York City; a cooling breeze rustled the leaves upon the trees while children rolled hoops and ran merrily about among the slowly promenading adults. What a microcosm of the new world this little park had become as people flocked in for this wonderful occasion, a slice of history revealed with the original owners there, the Lenni-Lenape Indians, a few Dutchmen—for they had been intrepid enough to attempt a colony here before the English overwhelmed them—Scotch and Irish who then came to settle, as well as immigrants from all the countries of Europe. And Indians and more Indians, Algonquin of all the five nations in their ceremonial finery of tall-feathered headdresses; Blackfeet and Crow from the west, Pueblo and Pima from even farther west, Aztec and Inca from the south, resplendent in their multicolored feather cloaks and ceremonial axes and war clubs—black rubber inserts replacing the deadly volcanic glass blades, Maya as well and members of the hundreds of other tribes and nations of South America. They strolled about, all of them, talking and pointing and enjoying the scene, buying ice cream, tortillas, hot dogs, tacos, and hot chillies from the vendors, balloons and toys, fireworks and flags galore. Here a dog ran barking chased by enthusiastic boys, there the first inebriate of the day was seized by one of the blue-clad New York's Finest and ushered into the waiting paddy wagon. All was as it should be and the world seemed a wonderful place.

Just before the City Hall steps the ceremonial reviewing stand had been set up, flag-draped and gilt-laden, with the microphones for the speakers in front and a lustily worked orchestra to the rear. Occasional political speakers had already alluded to the greatness of the occasion and their own superlative accomplishments, but were as little heeded, and in a sense provided the same sort of background music, as the musicians who played enthusiastically in between the speeches. This was of little more than passing interest to the crowd, though of course they enjoyed the melodious sounds, for they had come to see something else, something astonishing, something more memorable than politicos and piccolos. A train. *The* train, shining brilliantly in the sunshine. Sand had been spread right down the middle of Broadway and sleepers laid in the sand and tracks laid on the sleepers and not a soul had complained about the disruption of traffic because, during the night, the train had backed slowly down these tracks with the soldiers marching on each side to this spot to await the dawn. So there it was, the railings of the observation platform of the last car close to the reviewing stand, the gleaming cars stretching away down the tracks, glistening in the sun a deep, enameled ocean blue picked out with white about the windows, the official tunnel colors. Resplendent on each car in serifed and swirled gold letters was the proud legend: THE TRANSATLANTIC EXPRESS. Yet, fascinating as these cars were, the crowd was gathered thickest around the engine, pressing close to the barricades and the rigid lines of soldiers behind them, tall, strong men of the First Territorial Guards, impressive in their knee-high boots, Sam Browne belts, ceremonial tomahawks and busbies, bayonet-tipped rifles to the fore. What an engine this was! sister of the mighty Dreadnought which pulled the English section, Imperator by name and imperious in the splendor of its sleek, sterling silver-plated outer works. It was said that the engineer of this great machine had a doctorate from MIT, and he probably did since this engine was propelled by an atomic reactor as was Dreadnought.

Now the lucky passengers were arriving, their cars pulling up in the cleared area on the far side of the train for boarding, all of the rich, affluent, influential, beautiful people who had managed to obtain passage on this inaugural run. Cheers went up from the crowd as various prominent figures made their appearance and were ushered aboard. The clocks in the steeple of City Hall pointed closer and closer to the hour of departure and the excitement quickened as the final orotund syllables of the last orations rolled across the crowd. On the observation platform of the train the chairman of The Transatlantic Tunnel Board, Sir Winthrop, was making an address that those close to listened to with some interest, but which could not be heard in the rearmost reaches. Now there was a stirring in these outer ranks and a sudden chant, building up louder and louder until it all but drowned out the speaker.

"WASH-ING-TON! . . . WASH-ING-TON! . . . WASH-ING-TON!"

Louder and louder until the entire audience joined in and Sir Winthrop, bowing to the public will, smiled and waved Augustine Washington forward. Cheers echoed from the tall buildings on all sides so explosively that the well-fed pigeons rose up in a cloud and swooped over and around in a fluttering flock. The cheering went on, even more loudly if that were possible, until he raised his hands over his head, and then it died away. Now there was a real silence because they wanted to listen to him and remember what he said, for he was the man of the hour.

"Fellow Americans, this is an American day. This tunnel was dug and drilled and built by Americans, every mile of the way to the Azores Station. Americans died in its construction, but they died in a worthy cause, for we have done something that has never been done before, built something that never existed before, attained a victory never achieved before. This is your tunnel, your train, your success, for without the iron will of the American people behind it it would never have been done. I salute you and I thank you and I bid you good-bye."

After this there was no end to the cheering and even those closest in could not hear a syllable of the speech by the governor general of the American colonies, which perhaps was no tragedy after all. When he had finished, his lady stepped forward, said a few appropriate words, then broke a bottle of champagne against the train. It was only a stentorian blast from Imperator's whistle that brought silence at last, while those closest to the engine clapped hands to ears. Now sounds could be heard from the countless loudspeakers set on poles around the park, far distant sounds echoed by similar sounds here because these were broadcast radio signals sent directly from Paddington Station in London.

All aboard! was repeated by the conductor here, while the whistles of trainmen echoed identically on both sides of the Atlantic. So hushed were the people that only the train sounds could be heard now, the slamming of doors, shouted instructions and more whistles until finally, as the hands touched the hour, the releasing of brakes and the deep clatter of metal sounded as the two trains slid smoothly into motion. At this there was no restraining the crowd who cheered themselves hoarse and ran after the receding train, waving enthusiastically. Washington and the other dignitaries on the train waved back through the transparent canopy that had dropped into place over the observation platform. The trip had begun.

As soon as the train entered the tunnel under the Hudson River, Gus went to the bar car where he was greeted and applauded loudly and offered a good number of drinks, one or two of which he accepted. However, as soon as they had emerged in Queens, he excused himself and went to his seat and was pleasantly surprised to find the compartment empty; apparently the others were all in the crowded car he had just quitted. He was more than content then to sit looking out of the window as the little homes flashed by, then the meadows and farms of Long Island, while his thoughts and memories moved with the same kaleidoscopic quality. The labor done— it was hard to realize. All the men and the hundreds of thousands of hours of grueling effort that had gone into it, the tunnel sections and the rails, the underwater dredging, the submarine operations, the bridge, the railhead. All done. Faces and names swam in his memory, and if he had permitted himself to be tired, he would have been possessed by the most debilitating of fatigues. But he did not, for he was buoyed up by the reality of the success. A transatlantic tunnel at last!

With a rush of air the train dived into the tunnel mouth at Bridgehampton and out under the shallow Atlantic. Faster and faster, just as his thoughts went faster and faster, until they slowed and emerged in the sunlight of the Grand Banks Station, sliding into the station with the tubular cars of the deep-sea train section just across the platform. Normally the passengers would just stroll across to the other train while their containerized luggage was changed as well, a matter of a few short minutes. But today an hour had been allowed so the people aboard this inaugural trip could look around the artificial island. Gus had often enough seen the docks where the fishing boats unloaded their catch, the train yards and goods depots, so he crossed over and sat once again by himself, still wrapped in thought, while the chattering passengers returned and found their places, oohing at the luxurious appointments, ahing as the pneumatic doors whooshed into place and sealed themselves shut. Ponderous valves opened and the wheelless train floated forward into the long and shining steel chamber that was, in reality, an airlock. With the doors sealed and shut behind, the pumps labored and the air was removed from around them until the entire train hung unsuspended in a hard vacuum. Only then did the seal open at the other enu as the sleek silvery length slid into the evacuated tunnel beyond and began to pick up speed. There was no sensation inside the train as to how fast they were going, which was a good thing since, as they rushed down the slope of the Laurentian Cone, they went faster and faster until their top speed was near 2,000 miles an hour. Since there was nothing to see outside, the passengers soon lost interest and ordered drinks and snacks from the hurrying waiters and even broke out packs of cards for their amusement. But Gus could see the outside landscape in his memory, the covered trench on the ocean bed that hurtled toward the great valley of the Oceanographic Fracture Zone and across the floating bridge at its center. Good men had died here and now they were through the tunnel and over the bridge and past in an instant and already beginning the climb

186

up to the Azores Station, to once again glide into an airlock, only this time to have the air admitted from the outside.

Unknown to the passengers, both trains had been running under the guidance of the Brabbage computer which had apportioned certain amounts of time for the stops at the two intermediate stations, then had controlled train speeds as well so that now, as the American section of the Transatlantic Express slid slowly into the station, the English section was also approaching from the opposite direction, a beautifully timed mid-Atlantic meeting as both braked to a stop at the same instant.

Only a brief halt was scheduled here, for a few speeches, before the trains went their respective ways. Gus was looking out at the train opposite and at the waving crowd in its windows when there was a tap on his shoulder so that he turned to face a uniformed trainman.

"If you would come with me, Captain Washington."

There was an edge of concern to the man's voice that Gus caught instantly so that he nodded and rose at once, hoping that the others had not heard; but they were too involved in the novelty and the excitement to be very aware. The trainman led the way to the platform and Gus queried him at once.

"Not sure, sir, something about Sir Isambard. I was told to bring you at once."

They hurried across to the waiting train, and there was Iris who took him by the hand and led him down the passage out of earshot of the others.

"It's father. He has had another attack. And he asked to see you. The doctor is afraid that. . . ." She could not finish, and the tears so proudly held back until now burst forth. Gus touched his handkerchief lightly to her eyes as he said, "Take me to him."

Sir Isambard was alone in the compartment, except for the ministering physician, and the curtains were drawn. They let themselves in, and with a single look at the blanket-wrapped figure Gus knew that the matter was very grave indeed. The great engineer looked smaller now, and much older, as he lay with his eyes closed, his mouth slightly open and gasping for air; his lips had a definite bluish tinge to them. The physician was administering an injection to the flaccid arm, and they waited until he had finished before speaking.

"Daddy," said Iris, and could speak no more. His eyes opened slowly, and he looked at her for long seconds before speaking.

"Come in . . . both . . . come in. Doctor, I am weak . . . too weak. . . ."

"It is to be expected, sir, you must realize—"

"I realize I need something to sit me up . . . so I can speak. An injection, you know what I need."

"Any stimulants at this time would be definitely contraindicated."

"A fancy way of saying . . . they will kill me. Well, dying anyway . . . keep the machine running a bit longer is all I ask."

It took the physician but a moment to reach a decision—then he turned to his bag and prepared his medicines. They waited in silence while the injections were made and a touch of color washed through the sick man's cheeks.

"That is much better," said he, struggling to sit up.

"A false illusion," the doctor insisted. "Afterward—"

"Afterward the afterward," Sir Isambard said with some of his old manner returned. "I mean to see this inaugural run completed, doctor, and I'll do it if I have to be carried to the end on the tips of your infernal needles. Now clear out until we reach the Grand Banks Station where I'll need your aid to change trains." He waited until the door had closed, then turned to Gus. "I have played the fool, I can see that at last."

"Sir—"

"Do not interrupt. The tunnel is built, so our quarrels are at an end. If they ever existed, that is. As I come closer to my maker and that eternal moment of truth, I see that perhaps most of the troubles were caused by my denying your ability. If so, I am sorry. More important I feel that in my selfishness I have made two others suffer, and for this I am infinitely more sorry. At one time I believe you two wished to be wed. Do you still?" Iris answered for them both, with a quick nod

188

of her head, while her hand crept out and found Gus'. "Then so be it. Should have been done years ago."

"I could not leave you, father, nor will I. It is my decision."

"Nonsense. Marry him quick because you won't have to worry about caring for me much longer."

"You won't—!"

"Yes, I will. I had better. Man can only make a fool of himself on his deathbed, or admit he's been a fool. After that he had better die. Now send that physician fellow in, for I need a bit more help."

It was the mighty will inside that frail body that kept it going, for the attack should have felled him long since. Medicine helped, as medicine does, but it was the strong spirit that buoyed him up. At the Grand Banks Station a stretcher was waiting, and he was carried across to the other train while the passengers were rushed in their transfer—no sightseeing this time. Down into the tunnel again with Sir Isambard staring ahead fixedly, as though all his will were needed for the process of breathing and staying alive, which perhaps it was. A few minutes later the door opened and Gus looked up, then hurriedly climbed to his feet while Iris curtsied toward the young man who stood there.

"Please, don't bother," said he. "We were all concerned about Sir Isambard. How is he?"

"As good as might be expected, Your Highness," answered Gus.

"Fine. Captain Washington, if you have a moment, my mother would like to speak with you."

They left together, and Iris sat by her father, holding his cold hand, until Gus returned alone.

"Well?" Sir Isambard asked, his eyes opening at the sound of his entry.

"A very fine woman indeed. She congratulates us all on this work. Then she mentioned a knighthood—"

"Oh, Gus!"

"—which I refused, saying that there was something I wished more, something for my country. She understood completely. There has been much talk of independence since

189

the tunnel began and apparently the foreign minister, Lord Amis, has been after her continually, seeing more good in the colonies, she says, than he does in England at times. It seems that the wheels have been working below the surface, and there *will* be independence for America at last!"

"Oh, Gus, darling, then it has happened! What you have always wanted."

"Should have taken the knighthood, let the damned colonies take care of themselves."

Sir Isambard looked out of the window and fretted while they kissed long and passionately, until with a rush and a burst of light the dark tunnel ended and the green potato fields of Long Island appeared.

"So there," Sir Isambard said, with some satisfaction, stamping his cane on the floor. "So there! Transatlantic tunnel, under the entire ocean. A wonderful day."

He closed his eyes, smiling, and never opened them again.

ENVOI

Across the verdant Cheshire countryside the churchbells sounded their merry call, and anyone hearing them could not but smile at their pleasant sound. The church itself, an ancient graying Norman pile at Bulkeley, close by the ancestral Brassey manor of Bulkeley Old Hall, was so surrounded by hedge and flowers that only its tower was visible from the road. Behind it, bordered by the color and perfume of a carefully tended rose garden, was a small yard, and here three friends stood, the two men clasping hands.

"I can never thank you too much," said Gus Washington.

"Nonsense!" Alec Durell answered. "A distinct pleasure to stand up for you. Never been a best man before—in fact, haven't been in church for a donkey's years. In any case, plenty of perks involved. Bit of extra leave, more credit with my tailor for this morning suit, always needed one, chance to kiss the bride. In fact, think I'll try that again."

And he did while Iris' eyes shone and she laughed aloud, a vision in white and lace, happy as only brides can be.

"You are sure that you cannot stay for the reception?"

"Positive. Love to, of course, but duty calls. Signed off the old wombat of the *Queen Elizabeth*, too much of a milk run, back and forth across the Atlantic, might as well go under it in your tunnel like everyone else, for all I saw of it in my engine rooms. Took up my commission again, I did, Queen's shilling and all that, and they were damned glad to have me."

"Couldn't run the RAF without you." Gus laughed.

"Too true." He lowered his voice and looked around. "Strictly confidential now—you read the papers of course so you know about this spot of nastiness on the Continent. Count upon foreigners to make trouble any time. It's the

191

Saxons again, almost as bad as the Prussians, this time after the French. They have been trading shells back and forth across the Rhine which no one cares about as long as they blow up a few pigsties and such, but they hit one of the resort towns with their H.E., blew off the front of the hotel. Can't have that, British subjects staying there. Being evacuated, of course, but still. That's what battleships are for, as someone said."

They walked him as far as the garden gate, where, after shaking Gus' hand, he was presumptuous enough to kiss the bride again, something that, surprisingly enough, none of them seemed to mind.

"I'm on the *Invincible,* sister ship to the old *Courageous,* supposed to be identical but ten years more modern in every way. Four stokers in my engine room so we can feed the furnaces manually if the automatic equipment goes out. Fourteen steam turbines spinning her props, seven in each wing. The range is a secret, but it is really something, I can assure you, plenty of armament, light and heavy machine guns, small cannon in turrets on top of the twin tails, with two seven-inch recoilless cannon in a turret in her nose. Just wait until she flies along the old Rhine and puts a few bursts across their bows; they'll think twice about shelling Englishmen!"

He started down the lane, shoulders back in the best military manner, then turned to wave with a most unmilitary smile at the happy couple who stood, arms around each other, and called out, "Meant to congratulate you on the American independence. A good thing. Why don't you run for President, Gus? President Washington has rather an odd sound but a nice one. I bet you could do it. Go ahead!"

Whistling, he went around the turning and out of sight.